Something to Do with

LOVE

edited by

ANN PILLING

A LION BOOK

This selection copyright © Ann Pilling 1996

The Acknowledgments on page 192
constitute an extension of this copyright page

The authors assert the moral right
to be identified as the authors of these works

Published by
Lion Publishing plc
Sandy Lane West, Oxford, England
ISBN 0 7459 3114 6 (hbk)
ISBN 0 7459 3115 4 (pbk)
Albatross Books Pty Ltd
PO Box 320, Sutherland, NSW 2232, Australia
ISBN 0 7324 1526 8 (hbk)
ISBN 0 7324 1527 6 (pbk)

First hardback edition 1996
First paperback edition 1997
10 9 8 7 6 5 4 3 2 1 0

A catalogue record for this book is available
from the British Library

Printed and bound in Great Britain by
Caledonian International Book Manufacturing Ltd, Glasgow

Contents

*'I have been brought up, and I have
believed in the bottom of my heart that
you, God, had something to do with
love.'*

Sister Renate in *Unveiled* by Mary Loudon

Introduction

When first invited to edit this collection of short stories I resisted. The project meant 'Christian fiction' and I have never been sure what this is. If it is storytelling where a tract is dressed up as a novel, a romance, say, in which the heroine is saved instead of finding a lover, then I am not interested. When is a story art and when is it propaganda?

The American writer Flannery O'Connor had no doubts about the appropriateness of Christian fiction, feeling that the story mode was entirely appropriate for a believer because it is incarnational, because it gives flesh and blood to ideas and feelings. But the reader will be disappointed if, in these pages, he seeks a bland world-view where all is for the best in the best of all possible worlds. As O'Connor points out, any writer who cares about spiritual values is likely to take a dark view of contemporary society. The sharper the light of faith the more glaring the distortions a writer sees in life around him are likely to be.

The spaciousness of this view, and the bravery of it, gave me hope so, having said yes to the project, I started to read. I also made contact with those people whose work I admired whom I believed to have some religious faith. There were some interesting responses. One writer, who had embarked on a similar anthology and abandoned it, wished me better luck. Another understood my problem very well. 'Like you,' he wrote, 'I find the problem of Christian fiction a vexed one. I thought much about whether one should encourage or discourage an artistic identification with one's religious faith. If one encourages it, one puts off non-Christian readers and so fails to reach the unconverted; yet it is difficult to discourage it without appearing to disown one's beliefs.' It was a third response which persuaded me that this kind of collection was possible. 'Many of my stories fall into the category you mention but I think they do so in a roundabout and unobvious way.' I found myself responding to the unassuming diffidence of this. Here, possibly, was the key.

To all potential contributors I appealed for the same thing, for stories where there was 'a sense that, in the world you explore, spiritual things matter and are taken seriously, however you choose to develop your theme, and however open-ended the conclusion. I would like,' I went on, 'to find stories about the pain of belief as well as the joy, about doubt as well as certainty, about fun as well as solemnity.' Well, I found them, and here they are.

In *Unveiled* Mary Loudon talks with Renate, a German nun who, having belonged to the Hitler Youth, went on to witness unspeakable horrors in the Second World War. One day, in the trench, she said, 'I have been brought up, and I have believed in the bottom of my heart, that you, God, had something to do with love. But if this has anything to do with you, then I will have nothing to do with you.' Then she adds 'And I didn't finish that sentence. I unconsciously realized that the bottom of my life would drop out if I denied God.'**

In *The Sovereignty of Good* Iris Murdoch wrote 'all that consoles is fake.' 'We are so conscious of the tragedy of human existence,' comments Richard Harries, 'that we are suspicious of any good news. How can we convey a real sense of triumphant goodness? How can we talk about the crucifixion?... If it can be done that place where it can be done is in literature...'*** *All that consoles is fake.* But all art, all literature—these short stories—has the capacity to console; that is its highest good.

Apart from the fact that each of them is something to do with God and therefore 'something to do with love' I had looked for no further common theme. But in reading them again I see that, for all their diversity, there is, though sometimes only in the tiniest measure, *hope* in all of them. And because there is hope there is the possibility of good—and therefore, of consolation.

Ann Pilling
Oxford, December 1995

---

* 'Bloodwiser', Steve Turner (Strait Magazine, 1989)
** *Unveiled, Nuns Talking,* Mary Loudon (Chatto and Windus 1992)
***'Christian Faith and Literature', Richard Harries (A public lecture delivered to the Librarians' Christian Fellowship, October 1993)

The Meeting House

J A N E G A R D A M

*T*here should be nowhere less haunted than the Quaker meeting house on High Greenside above Calthorpedale in the Northwest.

To get there it is best to leave the car on the byroad and walk up through the fields, for there are six gates to open and shut before you reach the deserted village of Calthorpe, which stands on a round lake that is shallow and silver and clean and still. The hamlet's short street and its empty windows and door frames are nearly blocked with nettles, its roofs long gone missing. A century ago, poor farming people brought up broods of children here on tatie pies and rabbits and broth and, very occasionally, some pork. The pigsty—one lank pig to a village—lies above the ruined houses. Behind the pigsty you take a track up the fell until you hit a broad grass walk nibbled to a carpet by sheep since James I's time and before. You come to two stone buildings to the right of the walk in the tussocky grasses. They are attached, one house bigger than the other.

When you get near you see that the smaller building is

empty. A dark doorway gapes. There is not much roof left. But the creamy stone is bleached and washed clean by the weather and there are wild flowers and grasses round its feet.

The bigger building is one tall room within and is almost the oldest Quaker meeting house in England. George Fox himself is said to have preached here shortly after his vision of angels settling like flocks of birds on Pendle Hill. Its floor is the blue-white flagstones of the dale and there are three tiers of plain, dustless benches. The walls are dazzling white limewash and on a high stone shelf is a small paraffin stove and two now long-unused candlesticks. The Friends bring a medicine bottle of paraffin up the fell for making tea after worship but they don't bring candles, for the meeting house is used only on summer mornings now. It is a secure little place and bare. If walkers look through the clear glass in the windows they see nothing to steal.

The view from it is wonderfully beautiful and, as the Friends sit looking out through the windows and the open door across the dale to the purple mountains, a grassy breeze blows in; if Quakers believed in holy places this would be one of them. They do believe, however, in a duty to be responsible about property and thus it seems odd that the building alongside the meeting house should be derelict. But it had never been the corporate property of the Friends, being part of the estate of a local farming family who had been Friends for many generations and had used the little house as a lambing shed and springtime home of a shepherd who had doubled as the meeting house caretaker.

Those days are done. The farm has passed now to a consortium at York, the sheep are brought down to low pastures and shepherds today have motorbuggies and houses below the snow line. The meeting house caretaker was now Charlie Bainbridge, who had walked up to High Greenside once a week for years, at all seasons, and he had seen the smaller building left to fall gently down. Bainbridge, a huge old man, white-bearded and white-haired, was a still fellow who walked very upright without a stick even with snow on the ground. He said the long pull up to the meeting house was what had kept him healthy.

Hawks on the ridge had watched Bainbridge for years as he moved on a weekday morning across the valley floor, passing through the six field gates, fastening each one after himself; passing through the nettle-stuffed village, passing the muck-hard pigsty and away up beyond it to the broad grass track. On the common garth wall before the two buildings he sat down each week and ate his dinner out of a paper parcel and watched the weather coming and going. Larks and lambs in season, curlews at every season. Far too many rabbits. Disgraceful multitudes, he thought, remembering hard times and good stews of old. In winter there was often a stoat turned white, a rusty fox dipping a paw in snow. In April there were rainbows, often far below him and sometimes upside down. In May, a madness of cuckoos. A preserved and empty country.

He would consider the rain as it approached, watch the storms gather, the searchlights of sun piercing purple clouds and turning the fields to strobe-light, elf-light emerald. He sat waiting for the rain to reach him and wet him, the wind to knock him about. Until it did, he sat untroubled, like a beast. Then he got up and opened the meeting house door with the seven-inch iron key that lived under a stone, and plodded about inside maybe sweeping around a bit with the broom that lay under the benches. He looked out for cobwebs, trapped butterflies, signs of damp. Accumulated silence breathed from the building, wafted out on to the fell, swam in again like tides. Silence was at the root of Charlie's life.

So that when he was walking up one day and heard canned music he was jolted. He thought it could only be picnickers or bike boys cavorting about from over the west. They'd been seen about sometimes before. But then he saw that there were two big piles of rubble in front of the smaller building and clouds of lime dust floating in its dark doorway. Banging and crashing began to drown the music and then a dirty man came through the doorway carrying more rubbish and slung it on the tip. A child appeared, and then a very thin young grubby woman. The child was whining and the man aimed a kick at it. The woman swore at the man and the man said, 'Sod you. Shit.' The woman said, 'Leave it, will yer?'

Then the three stood looking at Bainbridge.

'Good day,' he said.

They said nothing. The man lit a cigarette.

'Can I help you?'

'Ye canna. We's 'ere. We's stoppin'.'

'Are you to do with them at York, then? The farming company?'

'We's 'omeless,' said the man. 'We's Tyneside.'

'See?' said the woman, and the baby stepped out of its plastic pants and defecated beside the rubbish.

'I come here,' said Bainbridge (in time), 'to see to the meeting house. We don't use it often but it's our property. We are Quakers. The Society of Friends.'

'No friends of us,' said the man. 'Ye'll not shift us. You can't force us.'

'We wouldn't force you,' said Bainbridge, 'it's not what we do. We don't have violence. But we have a right of way into the meeting house across the garth.'

'Not now you haven't,' said the man, setting light to the rubbish.

Bainbridge left. He had never been a talker. Once or twice he had come across such people as these and had tried to understand them. Sometimes he had watched things about homelessness on somebody's television set and had always given generously to appeals for them that dropped through his door. But confronting them had been shocking, as shocking as meeting fallen angels, bewildering, frightening, disgusting and against natural order. When the Elders of the Meeting went up to High Greenside a few days later to investigate, Bainbridge stayed at home and planted onions.

The squatters at once made their position quite clear: they were not going, a point they made clearer still to the owner of the building who came over before long in a Merc from Harrogate. The owner, however, was not deeply worried. When he found that the family was not an advance party of vagrants or new-age travellers or a pop-music festival that might take roots over his fields and settle there like George Fox's angels—fornicating, druggy, aggressive angels ruining pasture and stock—he said that at least the place was being used. The glass front door off a skip, the new metal windows set loose in the walls, the plastic chimneypot painted yellow and crazy tarpaulin slopped across the roof were matters for the National Park, not him. Carrying off an eighteenth-century rocking chair that the family had found in the rafters and also painted yellow, the owner said that he would of course have to tell the police.

'You do that.'

'I will. Oh, yes. Don't worry. I will,' he called and a Doberman who had been drooling and lolling with the baby in a broken chicken-wire playpen leapt at him with slippery turned-back lips, and man and chair fled down to the dead village.

'I'll give yer summat in rent when I'se in work, see? The wife's bad, see? She's had a tumour,' the man shouted after him. 'She likes it 'ere, see? Right?'

Next, a number of the Friends went up to explain to the family about the Sunday meetings and how, each week, they kept an hour of total silence at High Greenside. The music behind the glass door screamed and blared, the baby cried and it took a long time for the woman to answer their knocking. It was noon but she was in her nightdress.

'We sit in silence once a week. From ten-thirty until eleven-thirty on Sunday mornings. Only on six Sunday mornings. Only in summer. You are very welcome to join us.'

She said, 'Oh, yes. Yer comin' in?'

The flagstoned floor was still covered with lime dust and the sheep droppings of years had been heaped up with torn plastic bags of possessions—cracked shoes, rags, bottles, jars. There was a mattress with greasy coats across it and a new-looking television set and video recorder standing bewildered by the absence of electric sockets. In a little black hearth a fire of wormy sawn-up floorboards from the room above was burning, but the place was cold. The woman coughed, and behind the door that hid the stairs the Doberman boomed and clawed.

'You can't be very comfortable here.'

'It's OK.'

'We could help you. We have brought you a few groceries. And some runner beans and a stew.'

"E'd never.'

'Well, tell him we called. And about the silence on the Sundays.'

She wrapped a terrible matted cardigan more tightly around her bones. "E'd never listen. "E's that wild. One thing one minute, another the next.'

When they arrived the following Sunday the Friends found parts of old scrap-yard cars dragged across the garth and barbed wire fastened across their door. After negotiating all this and opening up the meeting house, they conferred, standing close together and thoughtful. The dog slavered and scraped inside the lambing-shed windows.

But seated soon on the familiar benches, their door open to a paradise morning, the dog quietened and the silence began. A different, answering silence from the house next door became almost distracting.

Or perhaps insolent; for the following Sunday the entry to the meeting house was blocked more thoroughly, this time with old roof beams, and, after they had struggled through these and silent worship had started, two transistors on different wavelengths were set outside on the party wall. An ill-tempered political argument fought with a programme of musical requests, both at full strength.

The next week it was a petrol-engine chain saw and for an hour its lilting scream, like cats in acid, seared the brain and ears and soul and a young Quaker who was a summer visitor from Leeds ran off down the hillside.

The noise was switched off the minute the hour ended and the clerk of the meeting, speaking slowly, said to the man lounging outside, 'By law, you know, you are meant to wear earmuffs when you're working one of these.'

The next week the man did wear earmuffs but the Quakers sat again in pain.

'What have you against us?' they asked as they locked up—now taking the key with them. Even Bainbridge looked shaken and drained. But the man said nothing.

The next week the saw broke down. The scream jolted and faded and died. It was a few minutes into the meeting and the man outside began to swear. He kicked and shouted, shouted and kicked, then stormed down to below the pigsty and shouted and kicked the tincan of his old pick-up van into action. Soon it could be heard exploding its way down through the fields.

The two transistors kept going when the sound of the pick-up had faded but their clack was now like balm and blessing after the saw; and a greater blessing followed, for soon they were switched off. The depth of the Quaker silence then was like hanging in clear water.

After a time, the child appeared in the open doorway quite naked—a queer, grey, dirty, sickly thing standing in the bright air. He tottered forward and flopped down and old Bessie Calvert, a gaunt stick herself, took him up on her lap, where he seemed to have no energy to do more than fall asleep.

When, in a few minutes, his mother stood in the doorway looking for him, Bessie moved a little and touched the seat beside her and the woman, again in her nightdress, threw her cigarette in the grass and came in. She sat sideways, twisted away from people, staring sulkily out of the door, but she sat, and when the car was heard returning she did not stir. And when the man and dog stood in the doorway she did not look at them. The dog's great chain was twice round the man's wrist and the chain rattled heavily as the dog dropped down to the ground, its chin on its paws. The dog sighed.

Then the man pulled the dog away and they both stood outside in the garth, the man leaning against the meeting house wall. 'Good day,' said the Quakers passing him by at the end of the house (there had been no tea-making this summer), holding out their hands as usual, one after another. As usual the hands were ignored but leaning against the wall the man gazed far away and said nothing. He looked very tired.

As they went off down his voice came bawling after them.

'—Next week, mind. Not an end of it. See what we do next week. Settle your silences. You'll not get rid of us. You's'll never be rid of us. We's after your place next.'

But the next week nobody was there. All were gone, the family, dog, car, television set, chain saw, the few poor sticks of furniture, the new padlock for the pathetic glass door that now stood open on the foul mattress, piles of nappy bags, flies and a mountain of sawn wood. A jam jar of harebells stood on a stone sill with a note under it saying, 'Sorry we had to go. We'd got started liking it up here.' In the paper the following Wednesday the Friends read that at about the time they had been reading the note the whole family and its dog had been killed in their wretched car on the M6 just below Tebay.

Quakers accept. Grief must be contained, translated. Friends do not as a rule extend themselves over funerals. But three of the Quakers from High Greenside did attend this one far away over in Cumbria and later on Charlie, Bessie and the clerk cleaned out the old lambing shed, removed the rubbish—the tarpaulin, the mattress—to the tip twelve miles off. They distributed the firewood and disposed of the sagging little chicken-wire playpen. They worked thoroughly and quietly but found themselves shaken beyond all expectation.

The playpen and the now withered harebells in the jar brought them close to weeping.

It was during the following winter that stories began. Walkers were puzzled by canned music that came from the High Greenside buildings and faded as they drew near. Fishermen down by the lake at night sometimes heard the barking of a great dog. Across the dale, people saw a light shining like a low star on the fell-side from where the empty buildings stood. After Christmas the Yorkshire farmer came back with his wife to inspect but had to turn away because the wife for no reason suddenly became very much afraid. Charlie Bainbridge was thankful that the snow came early and deep that year and stopped his weekly visit—not because of ghost talk, he had no belief in ghosts, but because the place now distressed him. When the snow melted he was in bed with chronic bronchitis brought on by the long indoor months. He grew better very slowly.

So that it was almost summer again before he got up to the meeting house once more. Rather thinner but still upright, he set off soon after his dinner one day in early May. He walked steadily, opening and shutting each gate as before, circling the silver shilling of the lake, through the bad village, up beyond the pigsty to the wide grass ride. It was a balmy, dreamy day. He was happy to be back. The bank rising to the far side of him was rich with cowslips. Rabbits as usual. A lark in a frenzy, so high he could scarcely see it. As he came near the two pale buildings he said, 'Well, now then. Very good. Swallows is back.'

He stopped and for the first time in many months looked down and across the sweep of the dale, the black and silver chain mail of the walls, the flashing sunlight. 'Grand day,' he said aloud and turned to find the Doberman standing before him across the path.

Then it was gone.

He looked over at the meeting house, but did not move. He heard a thread of music, then silence. He wondered if he heard laughter.

The silence grew around him again and he waited. He tried out some remarks to himself.

'Here's some puzzle,' was the first.

'I stand here,' was the second.

'Let's see now what it's all about,' was the third.

He walked forward to the common garth, opened the gate and looked into the derelict building. Nothing. The grass was growing again in the flagstoned floor. He walked along to the meeting house and looked through the windows. Nothing. Not a shadow. The place seemed to have wintered well. A clear light flowed in over the bare benches. All quite empty.

But then he saw them, all three together, on one of the long seats. It was not a vision, not a moment of revelation. There seemed nothing ghostly in it. The man had an arm along the back of the settle and the night-dressed, bare-foot woman had the child on her knee and had folded herself in against the man's shoulder. They looked very familiar to Charlie Bainbridge, like old friends or, as it might have been, his children. And yet changed: confident, peaceful, luminous, beyond harm, they were all gazing outward from the meeting house, intent and blissful in the quiet afternoon.

Lantern Stalk

TIM WINTON

*I*t was like playing soldiers. Egg began to see it was a game they could play without shame, out here in the bush. The sergeant major called 'Parade!' from back in the clearing, and the shadows of other school cadets crumped past as he tried to secure his ground-sheet tent in the twilight. His mother had insisted he come. He was bewildered. So many pieces of equipment. Everything proceeded too fast. The sergeant major's call became a scream. Egg lifted his block-of-wood boots and fell in with the others.

Officers appeared with searing torchbeams. They were teachers in fancy dress. The sergeant major brayed: 'At-tenhaargh!' Forty boys came raggedly to attention. It was the sound of a stampede. The sergeant major berated them. He was a school prefect and he played full back in the school team. Egg could smell dyed cotton and nugget and webbing and trees and earth. Stars were beginning to prick open the sky.

Captain Temby spoke. Even in the twilight Egg could see his beergut. He had felt Temby's sawn-off hockey stick on the back of his legs at PE more than once.

'Tonight, men, we're sending you on a lantern stalk.' A cheer; they liked to be called men. The sergeant major growled, 'For those of you too stupid to know what a lantern stalk is, I'll explain the aims and objectives of the exercise. You will be trucked out into the hills by the sea, and on the highest hill will be a lantern. Your task is to make it to the lantern, or inside the white circle of tape around the light, without being detected and tagged. Two men will be guarding the light. They have a fifteen-yard circle to cover. Ten officers and NCOs will be patrolling the area between you and the light. The aim is not to get seen, heard, smelt, felt or tasted. In short: not to get *caught*. At nine we will sound the trucks' horns to signal the end of the exercise. Be careful, for Chrissake.'

The darkness in the back of the truck was full of elbows and knees and the vegetable smell of sweat. Someone smoked. Next to Egg, Mukas and Roper told jokes.

Egg had found make-believe soldiering fun at first. Earlier in the year when he'd signed up there was the brand-new bag of kit: boots, uniforms, webbing, beret, and the trips to the rifle range at the edge of town where he tried to shoot cardboard men off the face of the embankment. He learned to pull apart an SLR rifle and an old Bren gun, to read maps and to use compasses. His mother said it would make a man of him, but his father looked at him sadly when he came home from parade, and didn't say a word. From his room at night he heard his parents arguing. His mother's voice was strong and rich. She spoke well. Egg's parents never got along. These days he saw little of his father who worked so hard in his office, seeing other husbands and wives. Each Saturday evening, Egg heard the chatter of his father's typewriter.

The phone rang night and day. Egg's mother and her friends drank sherry and spoke well in the living room. When she was angry, his mother called his father 'Reverend Eggleston' and he left the room looking whipped and pale. She kept Egg away from 'that church'. She broiled Egg with tears. 'I should have married a man,' she said. He hardly ever saw his mother and father together.

Egg was conscientious about homework. He stayed in his room a lot where it was peaceful. In the early evenings he jogged and bits of songs came to him in the rhythm of his breath. He wasn't exactly unhappy. He often thought about Stephanie Dew whom he'd caught looking at him twice in Maths. He smelt apricots in her hair when she passed him in the corridors. The proximity of her made him sad.

Some nights Egg had a dream. It was always the same: he was running up a staircase. Something terrible chased him. He could not see it or hear it but his bursting heart told him it was terrible. All along the staircase were doors padlocked against him. He hit them and sheered off them and staggered on, too scared to scream, upwards, up, twisting into the sky. Upon reaching the last step he woke. There was nothing beyond that last step, he was certain of it. Only cold space, some void to fall through forever.

'Hey, Egg, what's your plan?' Mukas asked. 'Hey, hey, Eggface!' Mukas pulled Egg's beret down over his eyes.

'Get out of it, slag-bag,' Egg said, shrugging away.

'What's your strategy? How you gonna get up to that lantern?'

'I dunno. Crawl like they said.'

'I reckon walk. Just get up and walk like you couldn't give a stiff. Reckon that's the trick.'

'Crawl, I reckon.'

'You'll never make it by nine o'clock.'

Egg shrugged in the dark. He didn't care; he was thinking about his parents. Probably, they would get divorced. He wished they could be normal. His mother was stronger than everyone else's mother. People said she wore the pants. And no one else's father was a minister.

With a whang, the tailgate of the truck swung down and someone bawled at them to get out. In the still darkness Egg heard other trucks in the distance. He got down and waited with the others by a wire fence. He smelt cow dung and wet oats. The ground oozed up wet chill. A long way off, the sea.

A light appeared small and fierce in the distance.

'All right, spread out,' the sergeant major said. 'It's a lot further than it looks. Don't let it out of your sight.'

A horn sounded, as though miles away.

'Go on, get going!'

Egg set out with Mukas and Roper, slouching along, boot-heavy. For a while there was nothing else in the night but the suggestion of crickets and the shuffle of bodies. No one spoke. They walked, hands in pockets, until a bark stopped them dead and a torch beam lanced across from the right.

'Middleton and Smythe—you're dead! Back to the truck.'

Egg fell to the ground. All around him, others did the same. He pressed into the sweet, wet earth, and he lay there listening to the others moving on. A stalk of grass poked his lip and he drew it into his mouth. For a while, he had the inclination to just go to sleep there and then, give the whole thing a miss. The whole exercise was stupid. Why the hell did his mother want him squirming up and down hills? He could be alone in his room now, or out in the streets jogging by uncurtained windows with the whole world baring itself to him.

He didn't know how long he lay there, but it was long after he stopped hearing others move past, long after he heard any movement at all. He would stick to crawling. With infinite care he began to belly-crawl to the left, clearing the way ahead before edging forward. Flank 'em, he thought vaguely. He crawled for a long time. The ground changed. In time he heard trees and began to make out their shapes against the sky. He picked his way through twigs and leaves until he rested behind a log with its smell of charcoal and ants. He was sore.

A cow bassooned softly. Egg lay on his back. The sky pressed down and it made him think that if someone knocked the chocks from the right corners, the whole lot would crash down and the world would be as it must once have been, with no margin between earth and space, no room for light or dark, plant or animal, no people. He had tried to write a class paper on the subject, but the teacher returned his opening paragraph with a suspicious glance.

Dew and cold reminded him that he had a lantern to stalk. He struck out again with a strange restlessness, sliding quickly over the even ground so that when he keeled out into nothing he wondered insanely whether he hadn't crawled off the edge of the world. He fell, filled himself with air, and had it driven from him a moment later when he hit the bottom of the washout hard enough to make white lights behind his eyes.

He got up quickly and fell down again. With his head on cold sand, he lay still and waited for the sky to settle. He was calm: it wasn't the first time he'd been badly winded. As before, he told himself he would not die, that breath would return. His heart felt engorged as it did when he dreamt his dream of the spiral staircase. He was afraid.

When he had his wind back, he rose and slewed about in the washout for a moment before aiming himself at the silhouette of the bank and scrabbling up. He came upon a fence which sang as he climbed through. He was tired of playing soldiers, so he walked brazenly through the shadows of a paddock, looking for the light on the hill and someone to blunder into for the sake of getting it over with. Only, he could not find the light. Crawling, as he had been, with his head to the ground, he hadn't seen the light for some time. He couldn't even remember when or where.

Egg marched on. He whistled. Quite suddenly, a light appeared. Below him, to the left. He galloped. Where had he been? He was above the lantern. Had he gone round behind? His boots thocked through wet, dung-thick, downsloping pasture. A dog barked. He stopped. It was a farmhouse. He was stalking the wrong light. Feeling reckless, he pressed ahead anyway. A dog spattered out of the dark to greet him, to blunt itself on his shins and whimper. Egg scuffed its cold slick coat and walked with it towards the light of the house. Lamplight streamed from a paned window, illuminating the shapes of parked vehicles. Egg moved carefully between flat-tops and utilities. In the house, people were singing, and to him it sounded like an old movie. He felt his heart fill again. He crept to the window and saw faces in the burnished light of a Tilley lamp.

Big rough-faced men and women with blunt chins and black eyes stood in a semicircle by the fireplace. A bearded man in a bib and brace held a white parcel in his arms. Egg saw the chequered smiles of the people. He saw their hands. A man near the end of the semicircle warmed the back of his legs by the fire. Tears glistened on his face. Egg was dumbfounded.

The big man with the white parcel looked around at those present and then to the window. Egg ducked. The dog pasted his face with its tongue. A door opened. Egg flattened himself on the ground.

'It's cold out.' The voice of a man. 'Come in by the fire.' Egg rolled over and looked up at the shadow.

'Come on, soldier.'

Inside there was quiet. Roots sputtered in the fireplace. Egg felt the faces coming to bear upon him. The man with the white bundle ushered him to a spot by the fire. Egg's uniform steamed. The bundle in the man's arms gave a tiny cough. A baby!

'Now,' said the man with the baby, 'we'll get on.'

Egg stole a look at the people in the room. They looked like farmers, people who knew what they thought. An old woman in a pink dressing-gown had two fluffy balls peering from between buttons. They were ducklings, he saw, and she was keeping them warm.

'What I was gunna say is that this kid is a bloody miracle. That little heart just suddenly starting to beat—that's a miracle. Tonight we claim God's promises for this baby... er... Bill, what's the name again?'

'It's,' the man with the tears cleared his throat, 'it's Sidney Robert James Maitland.'

'Like Bill said. And tonight we swear ourselves to the sacred duty of raising this kid up to hear God. That's what this is about. We love each other. We try. We look after each other in our way and that's miracle enough in this world. And now there's one more of us. Let's just hope the poor little bleeder can remember all his name.'

Everyone laughed and the man started to pray with the baby in his arms. Egg studied the still faces in the room, wondering who they all were. It was like a secret society, a Resistance meeting. The furniture in the room was pushed back against the walls: an old sofa, a card table, treadle sewing machine. The floorboards were polished. Egg felt warm and comfortable, but his heart remained engorged.

A loaf of bread came around the semicircle, and Egg, following the others' lead, broke a piece from it and ate it. The man holding the baby took the loaf from him and put it on the mantelpiece above the fire. A ceramic mug came around in the same manner and Egg drank from it. The liquid was warm as blood and it made his mouth shrivel, his belly glow. When Egg had drunk like the others, the mug went on the mantelpiece beside the loaf.

Then Egg saw that white bundle coming around, hand to hand, and his heart thickened and he felt it rising in his chest. Each person receiving the baby touched his face, looked into his eyes, and kissed him on the forehead. As it came to him, Egg felt panic. He was certain his arms would never bear the weight. The vanilla-smelling pupa slid into his arms, heavier even than he had expected. His knees creaked. He wanted to run away. How could such a thing be borne? It was insupportable. Someone coughed good-humouredly and Egg looked up.

'Serious business, soldier,' said the man in the bib and brace.

Egg glanced around at all the expectant faces. Some of them were rutted with tears. He freed one arm, reckless, and touched the infant's cheek, noticing his own blackened hands and clogged fingernails. He looked into the child's eyes. They were the colour of the night sky. Egg kissed the cool, sweet brow, then passed the baby to the man with a weak, faint sensation fluttering in him as though it had been an ammunition box he'd been holding and not a newborn.

'Amen,' said the man.

'Amen,' said the others.

'Beer and cake, then?' asked the man, holding his child for them all to see.

'Beer and cake!' they replied with a cheer and the room was suddenly full of movement. Egg stayed by the fire, almost dry. A thin woman in a mohair jumper put a glass of beer in his hands and a wedge of rainbow cake in the other, saying: 'You're a godfather, soldier.' Her smile surprised him. He was drinking beer. No one had asked him questions. A small man with no hair on the back of his head showed him how to play the spoons. The dog whined outside. Someone fiddled with an accordion. The night seemed so real. He could do nothing but stand and watch and listen and feel the panic of wonder. The beer was sour and cold as brass. His mouth rioted when he filled it with cake. He was dizzy; it was the light-headedness of the jogger. He was more than himself. He felt deeper and wider. He felt as though he was more.

Then the room went quiet. People cocked their heads to listen. Egg put his glass down. He heard the horn far out in the night.

'That's for me,' he said, going to the door. The man with the spoons saluted him. As Egg stepped out into the dark, the fat man who had presided over the ceremony put a hand on his shoulder and pushed a lump of rainbow cake into his hands.

'See you again, soldier.'

'Where?' The man shrugged.

Egg nodded.

Moving out across the paddock, Egg looked up to see the lantern away to his left, high up, miles away, it seemed, and to him it looked like a star descended from the night sky, from that darkness in his dream at the end of the staircase where he had never yet ventured. The locked fingers of his ribcage relaxed. He was not afraid. He stuffed rainbow cake into his pockets and began to run.

Except Ye Become...

A D R I A N   P L A S S

(A LITTLE GIRL runs up to a very satisfyingly policemanish sort of policeman.)

GIRL: *(Very breathless.)* 'Scuse me... oh, 'scuse me... Mr Policeman... Sir... 'scuse me!

PC: 'Allo, 'allo, 'allo. What's all this then, young feller-me-lad?

GIRL: I'm a girl! And I've found a flower.

PC: *(Laughs.)* You've found a flower, 'ave yer? I see. Well that's 'ardly a matter for 'er Majesty's police force now, is it?

GIRL: But you don't understand. It's not an ordinary flower—it's... it's... it's beautiful and it's tall and it's special and... please come and look!

PC: Well... I don't know...

GIRL: *(Rustles a paper bag.)* I'll give you a rhubarb and custard sweet if you do.

PC: Bribing a police officer, eh? All right then, just a quick look.

GIRL: It's over here. Come on!

PC: All right, all right. *(They move to the flower, looking up.)*

Well, blow me down!

GIRL: Don't you think it's lovely? I think it's lovely. Do you think it's lovely? I think it's...

PC: (*Interrupts worriedly.*) Oh, it's... er... lovely all right, but I am bound to point out in my official capacity that (*firmly*) it can't stop 'ere. Lovely and all that it may be, but it's blockin' the path and is therefore what we in the police force term a public nuisance. If it 'ad 'ad the sense to grow four feet away, over there, it might—I say might—'ave been all right. Apart from that, it's too blinkin' big!

GIRL: (*Aghast.*) Too blinkin' big for what?

PC: Well... it's obvious isn't it? It... well, you imagine one of them petals falling off and 'itting someone on the 'ead. Besides, you'll 'ave everyone walking along 'ere with their 'eads in the air not looking where they're going, and before you know where you are they'll be crashing into each other all over the place.

GIRL: Please... you can't hurt it. It's too...

PC: Let's 'ave a look at the old rule book. 'Ere we are. (*Clears throat.*) Section thirty-six, paragraph twelve, line eight. 'On encountering strange, abnormal or obstructive growths, the officer present shall summon a detachment of 'er majesty's armed forces, horticultural division, with three long blasts of his official whistle. He shall then relinquish 'is post to the military officer in charge.' Right! 'Ere goes! (*Blows whistle three times. Army squad enters—one officer and two men.*)

HIGGINS: Left, right, left, right. Halt!

PC: Ah! That was quick. Now, as you can see, (*laboriously*) we 'ave a case 'ere of what you might call...

OFFICER: (*Interrupting briskly.*) All right, Constable, carry on. The army is here now, we'll handle things.

Where's the flower? Ah, yes. Right, men. I don't know what it is, and I don't understand it, so I think we'd better blow it up. The enemy are devilish cunning, and I think what they've faced us with here is an unexploded flower. Corporal Higgins!

HIGGINS: Sah!

OFFICER: When I give the word you will place a small explosive charge at the base of the suspected object. Detonation of said charge will cause said device to explode, thus rendering said device harmless to the general public.

HIGGINS: Sah!

OFFICER: Private Hoggins!

HOGGINS: Sah!

OFFICER: Clear the area of all civilians until the danger's over. Shoot any who resist.

HOGGINS: Sah!

OFFICER: Right, men. Move!

HOGGINS: Right... back... back... Move along if you please, sir... Now, what have we here? I'm sorry, miss, but you can't stop here. (*Rising impatience.*) We have a job to do, miss, and that involves you moving right away from that... that flower. Will you let go of it? Right, if that's your attitude... 'Mission to speak, sah!

OFFICER: Carry on, man.

HOGGINS: Sah! This person, sah! Refuses to move, sah!

OFFICER: I don't think you understand the danger you're in, miss. When that thing goes up, it'll take you with it.

GIRL: But it's a flower, not a bomb... and even if it is a bomb, it's beautiful and frightening. You're ugly and frightening. Can't you please leave it alone?

OFFICER: Her mind's gone, Hoggins. Hold her back till we've finished.

HOGGINS: Sah! Right—you heard the officer—(*shouts*) Move!

GIRL: Ow! Let go! I think you're all horrid!

OFFICER: Right. Everybody down! Ready, Higgins?

HIGGINS: Sah!

OFFICER: Ignite on the word of command. Ignite! (*Small explosion.*)

GIRL: (*Running joyfully to the flower.*) It wasn't a bomb! It wasn't a bomb! You see! You see, sir! It wasn't a bomb! The flower's still there!

OFFICER: When you grow up, little girl, you'll hear about something called logic. If the army says that an object is a dangerous explosive device, and steps are taken to destroy the device, then logically said device can no longer exist. I see no flower. Do you see a flower, Higgins?

HIGGINS: No, sah!

OFFICER: Hoggins?

HOGGINS: No, sah!

GIRL: But it is still there. It is isn't it? You can see it, can't you? Oh, do look! (The soldiers prepare to move away.)

OFFICER: Right, men—let's move!

HIGGINS: Left, right, left, right... (*Fades into distance.*)

    (*Fade in to news.*)

NEWS-READER: Here is the news. In the heated debate in the commons tonight, Mr James Bland, the Minister for the Environment, sought to give assurances to the opposition spokesman on horticultural affairs that the large flower which has recently appeared in a small provincial town does not constitute a serious threat to national security. Mr Bland said that although contingency plans did exist for dealing with such a crisis on a national level, he had no reason to believe that the local authority concerned was not fully competent to deal with the situation, and that interference by central government in local affairs was not a feature of the manifesto that had brought his party to power. At the same time, he added, the government was fully up to date on the crisis and prepared to intervene if and when it became necessary. Replying to suggestions that the troops had in fact already tried and failed to subdue the flower, Mr Bland said that he was unable to comment for reasons of security. Meanwhile, observers report that the flower continues to flourish.

Now, the Middle East conflict, and after this week's fresh outbreak of hostilities... (*Fade out. Fade in —stirring, insistent documentary music is heard—to the introduction to the TV programme* Focus.)

PRESENTER: Good evening and welcome to *Focus*. Once again we are zooming in on a subject of current national concern. Our aim as always is to reveal the truth behind the rumours, to ask the important questions, and, if possible, to provide some of the answers. Tonight—it's the flower problem. Not flowers in general, but one flower in particular: the flower which stands behind me here. In a very short space of time this 'growth from below the ground' has threatened to undermine the very fabric of our society. Why has a single flower, admittedly an unusual one, given rise to so much controversy and debate? The alleged failure of the armed forces to deal with the situation raises serious questions about internal security, and indirectly the effectiveness of the present government. Should the flower go, or should it stay? People everywhere are demanding an answer.

Tonight, we have invited four experts to join us here on the spot—a comparative horticulturalist, a cabinet minister, a minister of the church, and a child psychologist—to give us their ideas on the implications of, and possible solutions to, this pressing problem. We are hoping—everyone is hoping—for some answers here tonight. But, first of all, could our children be in danger? For an answer to this question we turn to a child psychologist, Miss Olga Fink.

Psych.: I would like to say straightaway that I believe this flower to be a serious threat to the healthy mental development of those children who encounter it, and there are good reasons for this belief. I think everyone would agree that the flower is abnormal in many ways. For the developing child an encounter with such abnormality can grossly disturb and disrupt that perception of an ordered world which is so necessary to the maturing infant, and in some cases could cause serious damage. We can only achieve real security by seeing ourselves as units in a world where the laws of nature and human behaviour have never, and will never be, altered to any great extent. Clearly, then, the child who is suddenly exposed to such a phenomenon as this absurdity will begin to develop the dangerous notion that (*dramatic pause*)... things do not necessarily have to remain as they are. Throughout his life that child would be expecting, perhaps in serious cases, even hoping, for something more than the real world has to offer. Such an outlook can only lead to fantasy, depression and a paranoiac dissatisfaction with life as it really is. If we persist in allowing our children's minds to be filled with false ideals, they may become as obsessive as this child here, who originally found the flower and now seems hopelessly ensnared by the mutation. Unless I'm very much mistaken her responses will already be heavily conditioned by exposure to this plant. Let me show you what I mean. (*Approaches little girl as though visiting a dying relative.*) Little girl, what do you think about this flower? What do you see there?

GIRL: (*Puzzled.*) A flower.

PSYCH.: (*Indulgently.*) Of course, yes... but I mean, how does it make you feel inside?

GIRL: Happy.

PSYCH.: Happy?

GIRL: Yes, happy.

PSYCH.: Happy? Happy? (*Annoyed.*) What is happy? I want to know why you keep staring at this... thing.

GIRL: Because... it's beautiful. It's just... beautiful. I just love looking at it—it's *so* beautiful.

PSYCH.: But... (*Gives up in despair.*) As I thought, this sad little girl is already almost incapable of rational conversation. She sees only what appears before her, her feelings are dictated by her emotions, and her thinking is governed almost entirely by her thoughts. To use an old fashioned term, she is... simple. If this flower can have this effect in so short a time, we *must* decide how best to protect our children in the future. In my view, there can be no doubt—the flower must go!

PRESENTER: A grave warning indeed, and one which I am sure will cause parents everywhere to ask of the authorities, 'What are you going to do? What is the official view of the situation?' To answer these questions we have with us tonight the minister for the environment, the Right Honourable James Bland. Minister...

BLAND: Well, I think everyone will agree that there has already been too much beating about the bush on this issue. The time has come for somebody to make a committed stand on one side or the other. There has been quite enough talk—more than enough discussion. What is needed is the courage to put forward a definite viewpoint and stand by that viewpoint, whatever the consequences.

The flower must go! So say those who take that particular line, and I am in full agreement with any action which ensures that such an option remains a viable alternative. The arguments put forward in favour of preserving this plant are equalled in potency only by the highly respected views of those who do not take that particular stance. Let us not consider personal feelings, except to the extent that they guide us to a solution based on certain facts which must be ignored if the truth is to be served. The government is quite clear on this issue. We intend to pursue a firm policy of action until that policy is rendered obsolete by virtue of its inability to fulfil those objectives which caused it to be put forward in the first place. This kind of consistency, involving as it does a healthy refusal to equate theory with mere practice, will result in the flower staying within the boundaries of a situation which is defined by its insistence on a strong decision concerning the removal of restrictions on the flower's ultimate fate. Our position, then, is clear. We both oppose and support resistance to measures which are exclusive of either side of the argument. To those who do not welcome this kind of straight talking, we simply say, 'Leave it to those who do.' Thank you.

PRESENTER: Well I don't know what our viewers made of that, but I'd like to ask you a straight question, Mr Bland. Are you in favour of removing the flower, or allowing it to stay?

BLAND: That is exactly our position, yes.

PRESENTER: I'm sorry, Mr Bland, but can I press you a little further on that? What is the government going to do? What are your immediate plans? Where do you go from here?

BLAND: (*Pause.*) To the station. So sorry. Train to catch, must run, so sorry. All under control... (*Fades into distance.*)

PRESENTER: Well—so much for the government view. That was Mr James Bland, minister for the environment. Now, let's turn to the church for the spiritual angle, and I want to ask the Reverend William Cuthbert, vicar of the local church, how he sees the situation. Reverend, what do you think of this flower?

REVEREND: I must start by saying that I have personally examined this flower very carefully, and I have no hesitation in saying that it is one of the most beautiful things I have ever seen. The flower is, in fact, so stimulating (*a dangerous word for him?*) that I think it must be approached with care. The effect of such a bloom on both children and adults is very difficult to predict.

PRESENTER: What should we do?

REVEREND: I believe that a period of waiting is indicated. In, let us say, ten years' time, it should be more possible to assess the implications of this lovely object and perhaps even to give the go-ahead for free and general enjoyment of such unusual beauty.

PRESENTER: And in the meantime?

REVEREND: My suggestion is that the flower should certainly *not* be destroyed. Rather, let the church remove the plant and keep it carefully during the next decade in a secure part of one of our church gardens where it can neither harm nor be harmed, as might be the case if it were left out here in the open. At the end of that period the situation could be reviewed and the whole matter reconsidered.

PRESENTER: And in the meantime the flower would not be on view at all?

REVEREND: I am sure the church would have no objections to selected groups viewing the flower with the co-operation of the clergy involved. To this end one could prepare a viewing rota which might be concentrated on weekends, and also include one or two periods during the week.

PRESENTER: So what would the next move be?

REVEREND: I think that our priority must be to remove this beautiful thing from general circulation, both for its own safety and for the safety of those who may falsely interpret its meaning. We cannot be hasty in these matters. We may, (*pauses as he becomes increasingly absorbed by the flower*) like this little girl, feel... greatly attracted in a very simple way to the sheer loveliness of the flower, but perhaps in a sense (*comes to his senses*) she has started at the wrong end. We have a wonderful thing here. Let us not spoil it by relying too hastily on our initial responses to what we see. We have made one or two mistakes of this kind in the past. The result has been division, argument and disharmony. I hope that we have now learned our lesson. (*Increasing in confidence.*) We need to develop a universally accepted system of formal appreciation with regard to this flower before we allow passion or excitement to cloud the issue.

PRESENTER: Thank you very much, Reverend. Miss Fink, what do you think of the vicar's suggestion? Do you agree with him?

PSYCH.: Oh yes. If the flower is taken over by the church I think we can all stop worrying. It will be forgotten within weeks.

PRESENTER: Well, we seem to have an uneasy agreement there. Now, before we turn to our last speaker, I'll see if I can get a comment from the little girl who first found the flower. (*Goes to her.*) Hello, there! All the people listening would like to know what you think about this flower. Would you like to tell everybody?

GIRL: (*Pause.*) I think... I think... it's so lovely. I can't think of anything else to say.

PRESENTER: Okay, well now, you've listened to what all these people have been saying about what should be done with the flower. What do you think we should do with it?

GIRL: I think... perhaps... we should water it and then look at it some more.

PRESENTER: (*Touched.*) We should water it. I see. All right, you go and get some water while we go on with our programme. (*Girl leaves.*)

GIRL: All right, but you will look after it, won't you?

PRESENTER: Yes, yes of course. (*Turns to camera.*) If only it was that easy, but it's not. So let's turn to our last expert, Doctor Harry Winter, an internationally known comparative horticulturalist who has done much to bring horticulture to the people in a way that can be accepted and understood even by those who find it difficult to appreciate flowers of any kind. Doctor Winter...

WINTER: Right, if we could just gather round the flower. Good. Thank you. Well, you know, I think this whole thing has got rather out of hand, and I want to show you how a proper horticultural perspective will invalidate most of the myths which seem to surround this so-called flower. The fact is that in a very real sense, this flower simply cannot exist. It goes against all we know about plant growth. Let me say categorically that this is *not* a new species of plant. I've seen it all before. Everybody screams, 'New flower, new flower!' and within a few days it turns out be artificial or poisonous or freakish. This growth cannot exist in any know type of soil or climatic condition, and it will certainly never reproduce itself. And yet some people, including myself, do not feel that the flower should be totally destroyed. It has a certain... potential... charm, and I believe that any qualities that this plant possesses should be available to everybody. I suggest, therefore, that we preserve the flower, but in an acceptable form, in a form that will allow people to say, 'Yes! This is something I can enjoy without having to abandon my common sense.' Let me show what I mean. (*He produces a pair of garden shears and prepares to cut.*)

REVEREND: Are you sure that... (*Sound of first cut.*) Oh dear!

WINTER: If I just snip off this branch here... and this one... Cut a little more off this side... Now, let's shape these petals... and again... (*Lots of vigorous snips.*) There! I think that deals rather neatly with the situation. The flower now conforms to normal expectations, it can no longer harm the minds of little children, nor can it exhaust the wits of our politicians.

PRESENTER: Well, there we are. The flower problem seems to be a problem no more. Thank you, Mr Winter, Miss Fink, Reverend Cuthbert, and thank you for joining us.

From *Focus*, goodnight. (*Everybody leaves except the vicar.*)

PSYCH.: Are you coming, vicar?

REVEREND: Er, no... I think I'll just wait for... that is wait until... oh dear, oh dear, oh dear!

(*The little girl arrives back with her water.*)

GIRL: I've got the water... I... oh... oh no! (*Pause.*) Oh look, look at your poor, poor petals! Oh, I'm so sorry.

(*Silence.*)

REVEREND: I'm afraid we... I didn't think they'd actually hurt it. (*Pause.*) I wish... I wish I could have stopped them. I just didn't have the courage, I'm afraid. (*Pause.*) Do take your head out of your hands. Please don't cry.

GIRL: (*Raising her head.*) I'm not crying.

REVEREND: Oh..?

GIRL: I'm remembering.

REVEREND: Remembering...?

GIRL: My flower. I though someone might do something to it, so I looked and looked and looked at it so that I'd remember every bit of it.

REVEREND: And do you... remember every bit of it?

GIRL: Yes. I do. Every bit.

REVEREND: Hmmm... I'm afraid that although I remember it was very beautiful, the details are rather hazy. What with all the speakers and the discussions and... well. (*Pause.*) I wish I could see it again.

GIRL: Well...

REVEREND: Yes?

GIRL: I could tell you about it.

REVEREND: Would you? Please.

GIRL: Well, it was tall, and very unusual, and very, very pretty—and the colours—they were... they were blue and red and yellow. They were the best thing... (*They walk away hand in hand.*)

Jacob's Ladder

SARA MAITLAND

Jackie lived on the thirteenth floor. She ought not to live on the thirteenth floor because she had Estelle. Council Policy dictated that people with small children ought not to live on the thirteenth floor, but when she had requested a transfer they had offered her a flat the other side of town: she did not know anyone the other side of town, and she was frightened of moving so far from her mother and her friends, so she had turned the offer down. Later they offered her a flat that had only one bedroom; it was on the third floor of a block designed for, and predominantly occupied by, old people. During the half-hour that she had spent looking it over two different people asked her if she played loud music and one of them said they all hoped the child was quiet. Her friend Betty said, 'Oh stuff them!' but Jackie had a strong feeling that it would be more exhausting to have to say 'Stuff them' ten times a day, and not be able to escape from Estelle into the privacy of her own bedroom, than it would be to climb to the thirteenth floor. After that the Housing would not offer her another flat; she was known to be difficult.

There was a lift but sometimes it did not work and even when it did it frightened her. Going up she would become breathless with terror that it would stop and she would be stuck all night long in the little silver box; coming down she would get sweaty with fear that the ropes would snap and that Estelle would crash down thirteen floors and be pulped. She knew both these fears were stupid and she could not tell anyone about them. When people asked her why she walked up the stairs she said it was cheaper than aerobic classes. She had terrific legs anyway.

The stairs of the tower block were like this—she knew every step of them intimately—you came through the door on the ground floor and there was not very much light; there were windows but they were made of crinkled glass, reinforced with netting so they did not let much light in, even when they were clean which was not often. You could not see out of them, which was a pity since, after the sixth floor when the tower cleared the low-rise blocks around it, the view was spectacular. It was one of the compensations of her flat, once she had got there; she could stand in the evenings and watch the lights come on, the dark pool of the park lit with soft gold moons, the lights of the bridge far away like fairy lights on a Christmas tree and the cars on the motorway creating white comets as they came towards her and red flames as they went away.

The stairs rose through the grim gloom; nine steps then a small flat square, a right hand turn and nine steps. Four sets of nine steps to each floor; thirteen floors. Four hundred and sixty-eight steps. She thought that Estelle would grow up very good at sums, because as soon as she was able to walk Jackie had taught her to count them;

taught her her nine times table; taught her to take away almost any number from 468 to see how many stairs were left. Anything to while away those 468 stairs which ended each day in misery.

Jackie hated the stairs and was frightened of the lift and could not move flats and was pregnant. Jackie loved Estelle and got angry with her because there were so many stairs and each day Estelle had to be persuaded to walk up them.

Jackie hated the stairs, because they were so ugly. Once, in the night, someone had sprayed the whole wall between the tenth and the twelfth floor with a wild and wonderful design, a huge garish plant with luminous leaves and neon coloured flowers, carefully, beautifully sprayed on. She had skipped down the stairs next morning cheered for the day and full of glee. She and Estelle had tackled the stairs that evening almost with excitement, certainly with pleasure, but the walls had been stripped, there was a vague whiff of ammonia and detergent in the still air but all the flowers had gone, scrubbed off laboriously; but above them the scribbles, the obscenities and the NF daubings, not just ugly but frightening and dangerous as well, had been left.

The worst bit of the stairs were the floors between the fourth and the eleventh. Here the flats occupied two floors each, so that instead of having a door once every four sets of nine stairs, they had to climb eight sets without a break. Jackie told herself it did not matter; that she seldom left the stairwell for the long landings beyond the doors, but it did matter. On bad days she would feel that they were trapped, that they would be climbing forever through the stagnant air; glared at in the gloom by hatred and violence and squalor and exhaustion.

So the first time that Estelle laughed Jackie was surprised but pleased. They were struggling up the stairs between the ninth and tenth floors; it was a wet November evening and they were both tired. They made the right turn on the second set of nine stairs and Estelle giggled. Jackie looked down; her lovely three year old with her huge eyes was looking up towards the next little landing and giggling. Estelle was only three and still could not explain things very well; Jackie knew better than to ask her what the joke was. But she took heart, smiled back and they managed the last three floors with some spirit.

That night, warmed by her daughter's happiness, she rebraided Estelle's hair, the way her grandmother had done hers when she was small and sent her off to nursery the next morning with twenty-three tiny bright red satin ribbons bobbing at the end of the corn rows.

Jackie forgot the laughter until the next evening when it happened again; and every evening that week. They would be plodding up the stairs tiredly, with Estelle limp and whiney with exhaustion and then they would turn the corner between the ninth and tenth floors and Estelle would perk up. By the end of the week she would even slip her hand from her mother's and push on ahead, and when Jackie caught up with her, there she would be standing on the steps looking upwards and laughing.

It began to irritate Jackie—an irritation compounded of her own exhaustion and joylessness, of bafflement and of concern. The child was old enough to know that walking up all those stairs was not funny. It was time she faced up to the difficulties that her mother had to endure. She had sacrificed her whole life for that little girl and she got nothing back except crazy gigglings.

There was no time in this life to stand on staircases and laugh.

Estelle was a lovely little girl, happy and contented, pretty as a picture and reasonably well behaved. But this abandoned laughter reminded Jackie too much of Estelle's father, who had always been laughing and had laughed his way out of the house and out of Jackie's life three weeks after Estelle had been born. No sense. She could not bear to raise a child with no sense. Sense was what you needed to survive. So although she was glad the child was happy, indeed was radiant, she worried, and the worry along with all her other worries, made her irritable. Her irritation, however, did not stop the laughter, which over the course of the days became wild, hilarious, echoing off the walls of the stairwell, filling the square space with music.

After a week Jackie could not bear it any longer and steeled herself to use the lift: she thought about it all day, ordering herself to keep calm and not to frighten Estelle. By the time they had risen to the thirteenth floor she was sweating, her palms were cut by her own nails pressing into them, her lips bleeding slightly from the effort of not screaming in front of her child, and Estelle was crying. The evening was dreadful; Estelle wouldn't eat her tea, wouldn't play, and for the first time in her life wouldn't give her mother a good-night kiss. Jackie went to bed with a back ache, with the flavour of sick in her mouth, and with a surging panic about what she was doing with a small child and another on the way. She could not sleep.

The next evening she surrendered. It was raining. Estelle, restored to her normal energetic serenity, led the homebound expedition, turned in the ground floor lobby, away from the lift and into the stairwell, they started climbing, Estelle first, eagerly, and Jackie trudging after her defeated, weary, despairing.

After they passed the door to the fourth floor landing Jackie knew they had entered hell. The stench was overwhelming, stale puddles darkening in corners. On one of the small turns between the fifth and sixth floors someone's used works were lying abandoned. Estelle did not seem to notice, but Jackie felt the cold terror—she had not used drugs since she got pregnant with Estelle, but the shadow was there, waiting to pounce.

Her back ached. She did not need another child. She did not need this staircase. She did not need this life.

They climbed slowly; and as they came round the corner of the second nine steps between the ninth and tenth floors, Estelle stopped, looked up and started laughing. It was too much. Jackie grabbed her child and could hear her own voice from far away, ugly, dangerous, but she could not stop it. She was shaking Estelle and shouting, shouting 'Shut up! Just shut up!', and worse things that she knew she would be sorry for later but could not stop now. There was nothing to laugh at. She was shouting and crying and shaking her daughter, helpless in her rage.

Then, abruptly, it was over. They were both crying. 'I'm sorry,' Jackie said holding Estelle close, 'I'm sorry, I'm sorry.'

'Help,' she cried inwardly, 'somebody help me.'

She sat down on the dirty step and held Estelle in her arms, crying into her warm shoulder. Estelle was hugging her, hugging her not as a three year old hugs, but as a mother hugs. Her tears stopped suddenly. Jackie was aware that the child had raised her head and was staring up the staircase. With the tears still on her little fat cheeks a smile began to dawn in the darkness.

'Mummy, look,' she said.

Jackie turned awkwardly, her arms still around her precious baby. In the corner, where the stairs turned again in their inexorable climb, there was an angel standing and grinning at Estelle.

It was a slightly unexpected angel, rather small and wearing a bright pink track suit and silver trainers, but you could tell: without doubt it was an angel. It wore a diamanté halo on its neatly corn-rowed head and it had proper silky wings, each strand of the wings had been braided and tidily finished off with a tiny bright red satin ribbon bow. She smiled in a kindly sort of way at Jackie, but spoke to Estelle, 'About time too, don't you think, pet?'

Jackie thought she was frightened, but found that in fact she was smiling. No, she wasn't smiling, she was grinning, she was grinning and giggling. From somewhere deep inside her she heard a laugh, and it grew, swelling out of her, golden, deeper-toned but in perfect harmony with Estelle's bell-like laugh. The two of them were sitting on the stairwell hugging each other and laughing.

'Is she yours?' Jackie asked Estelle.

'No,' said Estelle, puzzled by the question.

'Certainly not,' said the angel, a little severely, 'I'm just using the staircase.'

'Silly angel,' said Estelle.

'Of course,' said the angel, and laughed too.

All three of them laughed, filling the ugly stairwell with music.

The angel passed them on her way down smelling faintly of Chanel perfume and cinnamon. Estelle and

Jackie climbed on up. Jackie noticed that her back no longer ached.

After tea they stood on the balcony and enjoyed the best view in the city. The lights sparkled like diamanté along with river; there were red ribbons from the cars going somewhere else, and silver streaks from the cars rushing towards them on the motorway.

Jackie said to Estelle, 'We're going to have a baby. What shall we call her? Do you think Hope's a pretty name?'

'Can't we have a brother?' said Estelle, not very interested.

'We could call him Hope then,' said Jackie.

'Silly Mummy,' said Estelle.

They both laughed, and all the angels using the staircase as a short cut laughed with them.

Even the Mice Know

MICHAEL CARSON

*T*he old woman entered the elevator on the twenty-ninth floor just as Ed Welch had started to think he was going to be alone the whole way down. She entered slowly, leaning on a walking frame. Ed Welch held the Door Open button for her.

Once inside, she spoke through her smile across the elevator as it plummeted to earth.

'Only five more days,' she said.

Her smile cleared her face of age as a high wind will a street of autumn leaves. Ed Welch watched the smile, saw the old lady as she might have been half a century ago, at once compared the sight of her, unfavourably, with his own soul—but completely missed what she had said.

For Ed Welch had been feeling even more disturbed since getting into the elevator; wondering if the elevator was, in fact, still in control and suspended from the metal rope which yo-yoed it up and down the building a thousand times a day—or whether, just for him on this day, a day when by rights it should not matter, the elevator had decided to part company from its helpmate, the wire. When the old woman spoke he had been wondering what happened to bodies after they had undergone the fall from twenty-nine floors to the ground. If he jumped high in the air round about the third floor, would he come out unscathed?

'Oh yes?' he replied.

The old lady dropped her smile and became old again. Ed Welch attempted to smile at her, but it did no good. No, he thought. Sure as eggs are eggs he'd be scrambled by the impact just like everybody else. He shivered.

'Yes, only five more days.'

Of course! Of course he knew exactly what the old woman was referring to. It was so obvious. Every street in San Francisco proclaimed it: lights on all the buildings; the piles of pointless poinsettias everywhere; the video store outside the apartment building showing a film in its window, hour after hour, of a log fire burning, with stockings hung. (How would Santa make his way through that inferno?) Yes, all things proclaimed it. But Ed Welch, still apprehensive about the lift, despairing, feeling hatred gobbling up the man he had been a mere week before, pressed his thick-lensed spectacles against the bridge of his nose and decided to be opaque with the old woman. He smiled and said, 'Really?' noting that the lift had come to the sixth floor.

It would soon be time to jump for it if any time was the time to jump. But he couldn't tell the old woman to jump. He decided not to jump. He would let whatever would happen happen. He would be dying in good company.

She was looking at him quizzically, both her hands resting on the walking frame. She was small and slightly stooped, with a face now like an abrupt, efficient housekeeper hedgehog in a children's story.

The elevator came harmlessly to rest at the first floor as it always had and he hoped for the old woman's sake if not his own, please God, always would. The doors opened. Ed Welch walked out of the elevator with her, measuring his pace, guarding her like some Victorian angel minding a child across a river. She gazed up at him once or twice, a child wondering what this strange apparition was up to.

At last they reached the centre of the lobby of the apartment building. There, she turned to—or rather on—him and said, 'Yes. Five more days. Five more!' as if she were addressing somebody very deaf or very dense.

'Sorry?' he asked, enjoying the game he was playing.

The old woman sighed and shook her head slowly towards the walking frame. 'You mean you don't know? You really don't know?' she asked him.

'Know what?' he asked, thinking of Scrooge and the empty apartment he had left behind on the forty-seventh floor, his depression suddenly back—where had it gone while he had been helping the old lady?—and pounding like a migraine.

She continued on across the lobby and fixed him with a hard stare. 'I have to check my mailbox. Goodbye.'

'I'd offer to check it for you but I know you want the exercise,' he said.

'Well, I'm glad you know something,' replied the old woman, wounding him strangely, making him lift his hand in protest, to protect himself. But then he deflected his arm and made his hand stroke his unshaven chin instead.

He left her there. Albert the doorman opened the door for him and wished him the compliments of the season. Ed Welch smiled and thought he ought to remember to tip the man before he left.

Outside it would soon be getting dark. The city had been swathed in low cloud all day but now, out towards the Golden Gate bridge, he saw that the sun was about to put in a brief appearance on the horizon. Just above it the bank of cloud ended and a thin strip of blue promised a fine day on the morrow. Out in the Pacific everything would be bright and golden. He thought of his ticket. Tomorrow morning he would be going west—though he did not want to; could hardly bear to.

'Now, what do I have to do?' he asked himself.

He knew there was a lot to be done. He fumbled about in the untidy drawers of his brain marked 'wants, needs, whims', extracted from them a list of what to do, get and enquire about, trying to place everything in some sort of order of priority.

He passed the Bon Appetit supermarket and thought of the old woman. Had she arrived at her mailbox yet? She would probably be bound for the supermarket but it would take her an age. He wondered if he should have offered to do her shopping for her but was sure that the tough old bird would have taken such an offer amiss.

Anyway, he wished her well. She was the first human being he had spoken to since it had happened.

Then he saw himself on his plane heading out and thinking of her as the plane nosed towards Singapore. He knew he would think of her then. Better to think of a sweet old woman than of...

He walked up Sacramento Street, passing young business-people. He did not know why, but they seemed dangerous, somehow threatening, to him in their sharp suits. They had hardly a glance for him. He had had his day and looked it.

'Spare a quarter for a cup of coffee, sir.'

Ed Welch was on top of the beggar before he saw him. He fumbled in his pockets, saying, 'Er... well...' as he did so, firmly focusing his gaze on the sidewalk at his feet. Almost in a panic he searched for change, finally finding some in the pocket which held his revolver. He took some out and tossed it into the man's paper cup. Then he walked on hastily.

As he did so, he heard, 'Compliments of the season to you, sir! My heartfelt thanks, sir!' enunciated by a voice that would have done justice to a reading of Walt Whitman in a large auditorium.

He half turned and nodded. But if the beggar noticed he did not say anything else.

Ed Welch thought how embarrassing it was to show small acts of generosity. The money parted with was by a long way the least of it. It hardly figured at all in fact. No, rather, the generosity, the virtue of giving to someone in need in a public place, was to scramble for the coins while under the gaze of a maybe-critical populace; then, having found the coins, to make the quick dart to the recipient while still under public scrutiny. Did those passers-by think him silly, soft, or, worst of all, a Holy Joe? Then, of course, did the recipient think he had been generous enough? And what about God?

He remembered one single, uncluttered act of charity while working in Madras years before. At his filling station, every Monday, a woman in a tattered, oily sari had filled up his car. Every Monday he said 'Fill her up!'

and every week she had done so and then charged him five rupees more than she should have done. Yet every week he donated those five rupees to the woman, knowing as he did so that she probably thought him a fool. He never tipped the woman. Indeed he was always rather brusque with her and each time he drove away from the filling station he felt as if he had been cheated. The act did not make him feel good—and that had to be good.

He found that he had walked his way too far up Sacramento. He stopped, trying to recall what he was seeking. Was it a want, a need, or a whim? He could not remember but reasoned that if he could not remember it was, in all probability, a whim. He turned on his heel and walked back down the street, distracted now by the sight of the chockfull Bay Bridge hopping over the East Bay to Oakland. Gertrude Stein, he recalled, had said that the trouble with Oakland was that there was no 'there' there—whatever that meant.

'Spare a quarter for a cup of coffee, sir!'

'You've already done me,' Ed Welch replied, but not loud enough for anyone but himself to hear. Then he repeated the phrase to the fog above him that furled and foamed and blocked the Ears of the God he now addressed. He smiled wryly.

He had walked on past the man but suddenly stopped, and searched his pockets again. He retraced his steps and gave the man all the change he was able to find. He gazed at the paper cup doggedly.

'Thank you again, sir. Good luck to you! May the New Year bring joy to you and your family.'

'I haven't got a family, I'm afraid, but thank you for your compliments. I wish you all the best too.'

The beggar did not say anything further and Ed turned away and continued down Sacramento and then turned on to Sansome Street, trying to think of his important wants and needs.

He arrived at Market Street but was still unable to remember a single thing he had to do. He shrugged inwardly and decided that that must mean that there really was nothing further to be done. Then he nodded at the truth of that. He had emptied everything out. All traces of his dead family had been packed up and collected by Goodwill. What did he need on his journey? You could buy paper handkerchiefs in Singapore, couldn't you? Probably some enterprising vendor would be selling them outside the mortuary. What did he need—apart from a wife and two grown daughters whom he had been about to 'get off his hands'? Well, they were off his hands now, weren't they? Were they? He found that he had brought his fingers up to his face and was sniffing them.

It would be hard getting on to the plane. He would, no doubt, feel terrible when confronted with the plastic wall covering of the cabin and the seats that must be the same kind of seat his wife and daughters had sat in, been strapped into and then clung to and wept against and then screamed and despaired in. Had they panicked? Had they rushed around the cabin in the minutes between the emergency and the crash? Or had they sat holding hands across the three seats bidding farewell and watching the clouds outside—tears streaming—as the plane plummeted? Had they thought of him?

On second thoughts, he decided, he did need something. He went into a drug-store and bought a packet of double-sided razor blades. He found his face would not function to ask the salesgirl the price. His mouth was dry, as if stuffed full of powdered bone.

Then, back on Market Street, he watched the rush-hour traffic for a minute, standing stock still and panting like a dog.

'Is everything all right, sir?' a young woman asked him.

He nodded to the woman. 'Yes. Thank you. You see... it's just... I must go home.' And he fled back along Battery Street towards the apartment building.

He had recovered himself by the time he passed Bon Appetit; had even managed to remember all the things he had forgotten to do, though he did not care that he had forgotten.

And he was not in the least surprised when he saw the old woman struggling back from the supermarket, crammed bags hanging from her walking frame.

'Remember me?' he asked her.

'A guy with total amnesia is not that easy to forget,' replied the old woman. She stopped for a rest.

'It's taken you a while to do your marketing,' he said.

'I've got time.'

'Now you must let me help you carry your parcels. They must be slowing you down.'

He reached over to take one of the bags but she slapped his hand.

'No!' she almost shouted, and startled him.

'But surely...'

'Do you know yet?'

'Know what?'

'What everybody knows.'

He was back in the game begun in the lift. 'No. What?'

'You must know! Why even the mice know!'

She looked concerned, almost on the verge of tears. He decided that the game had gone far enough. She really did think that he didn't know. He *did* know. The trouble was that he did not feel.

'Yes, Christmas is coming,' he said flatly.

'Right. You can carry my things for me now, though I warn you, you're in for a slow walk home.'

He took the two heavy bags from the walking frame and walked beside her back towards the apartment building. He bent towards her like a willow bends over a stream and listened to her speaking. And as he listened the weight of the last week—of all of his fifty-five years—lifted itself off him, lightened him, as his lifting of the bags had lightened the walking frame. His loneliness and despair and wild plans for vengeance dissolved as he listened and took tiny baby-steps beside the old woman.

'I must leave you now,' she told him as the lift opened at her floor.

He nodded, held the Door Open button for her and she slowly walked out of his life. The lift door drew shut behind her.

Back in his empty apartment he took the revolver from his pocket, wrapped it in several plastic bags and dropped it down the refuse chute. Then he sent the razor blades the same way and walked out on to his balcony.

The clock on the Ferry Building, far below him to his left, struck six and then the bells launched into a Christmas carol to which he could not put a name.

'I will go to Singapore and identify the bodies. Then I shall return and help the old woman with her shopping.'

He laughed at the foolishness of the idea but consoled himself that the idea was less foolish than others he had had in the past week.

Then, quite suddenly, completely taken by surprise as he leaned against the guard-rail gazing down and out over the Ferry Buildings and the Bay Bridge and the dark water and the lights of Oakland, he was weeping. The bells finished the carol and he could hear himself bawling, like an infant, feel the snot pouring out of his nose, as tears flooded from his eyes and down his face; plummeting earthward—past all the balconies below his and on to the sidewalk where old women struggle and beggars ask for aid and where, perhaps, when everyone is tucked up in their beds, the mice come out and tell one another what they know.

Sister Malone
and the Obstinate Man

RUMER GODDEN

*S*ister Malone had an extraordinary capacity for faith. She was in charge of the Out-Patients in the Elizabeth Scott Memorial Hospital for Women and Children, in a suburb of Calcutta, run by the Anglican order to which she belonged. She needed her faith; terrible things passed under her hands.

All sorts of patients came in all sorts of vehicles, rickshaws, curtained or uncurtained, hired carriages that had shutters to close them—they looked like boxes on wheels; a taxi with an accident case lying on the floor so that the blood should not soil the cushions, perhaps a case that the taxi itself had run over—it was astonishing how often taxis did run over patients. A few came pillion on a bicycle; some could walk and some were carried; there were fathers carrying children, mothers carrying children, small children carrying smaller children. Sometimes whole families brought one patient; servants of the rich brought their charges, or their mistress, or brought themselves. There were Hindu women in purdah, Moslem women in *burkas*, white coverings like tents that hid them from their heads to the ground, and hill women walking free as did the beggar women. There were high-caste Brahmins and untouchables; all colours of skin, dark, brown, pale; and all sorts of flesh, soft, pampered, thin, withered, sweet, ill-treated.

There were diseased women, diseased children, burned children; even more often there were tubercular children, deep and dreadful tubercular abscesses on breasts and groins and armpits were common. There was a great deal of ophthalmia and rickets and scabies, cases of leprosy and poisoning and fevers; there were broken bones made septic by neglect or wounds treated with dung and oozing pus. There were bites from rabid dogs and sometimes bites from human beings and, like a repeated chorus, always, burns and tuberculosis. This was not the result of famine or of war, this was everyday, an everyday average in one of the departments of one of the hospitals in the city, an everyday sample of its pain and poverty and indifference and the misuse of its human beings. Sister Malone certainly needed that extraordinary faith.

Most of the sisters who were detailed to help her asked to be transferred after a few months; they became haunted and could not sleep. Sister Malone had worked here for seven years. 'Sister, how *can* you? I... you... I... I cannot bear it, Sister.'

'You must have faith,' said Sister Malone, and she quoted, as she had quoted a hundred hundred times: ' "And now abideth faith, hope and love, these three." '

She paused, gazing through the thick lenses of her glasses that made her look a little blind. 'God forgive me for differing,' said Sister Malone, 'but you know, dear, the greatest to me is faith.' Then a question, a little persistent question, sometimes reared its head: was Sister Malone lacking a little in love, a little unsympathetic? Surely not. She was so splendid with the patients, though there was one small sign that no one noticed; the patients called her Didi—'Sister'; she spoke of them as 'they', a race apart. 'If only,' she said—and she said so continually—'if only they could have a little faith for themselves!'

She tried to give it to them. In the corner of the treatment room there was a shelf on which lay paper-covered gospels translated into Hindi, Bengali, Urdu, and Gurkhali. Sister Malone gave one to every patient. She walked sincerely in what she believed to be the footsteps of Christ. 'It is seeing so much eye-trouble and lepers,' said Sister Malone, 'that makes it so very vivid. Of course Our Lord knew that lepers are not nearly as infectious as is commonly thought. People are so mistaken about lepers,' said Sister Malone earnestly. 'I have always thought it a pity to use the word "unclean". I have known some quite clean lepers. Think of it, dear,' she had said wistfully, 'He put out His hand and touched them and made them whole. So quick! Here it is such a slow, slow business. But of course,' she said and sighed, 'they need to have faith.'

Sister Malone was a small firm flat woman. Her hands probably knew more of actual India, had probed it more deeply, than any politician's brain. These implements—yes, implements, because the dictionary definition of 'implement' is 'whatever may fill up or supply a want' and that was a good description of Sister Malone's hands—these implements were small and flat and firm; they needed to be firm.

At eight o'clock one blinding white-hot morning in June, just before the break of the rains, Sister Malone, Sister Shelley, and Sister Latch walked into the treatment room. Over their white habits, black girdles and the ebony crucifixes on their breasts they put on aprons; the crosses showed through the bibs. They turned up their sleeves and went across to the sink, where the tap ran perpetually, to scrub their hands, nails, wrists, and forearms, and afterwards immerse them in a basin of water and disinfectant.

Sister Shelley and Sister Latch were the two nuns detailed to help in the treatment room at that time. Sister Shelley was pale, her face drawn and sensitive between the bands of her coif; her eyes looked as if she had a headache. Sister Latch was newly out from home. Her steps were firm and certain; her pink face was made pinker by the heat; her body, well fed, solid, was already sweating through her clothes. She was cheerful, observant, sensible and interested. It was her first morning with the Out-Patients.

Through the window, as she scrubbed her hands, she noticed two little green parakeets tumbling in a gul-mohr tree. She would have liked to draw the other sisters' attention to them but she did not dare.

The Out-Patients was divided into the doctor's room, the waiting-hall, the dispensary, and the treatment room, which had a small examination room leading off it. The patients waited in the hall, which was furnished only with the pictures; they sat in rows on the floor. Each went to the doctor in turn and then, with their tickets in their hands, were admitted to the dispensary for free medicine, or to the treatment room for dressings, examination, slight operations, or emergency treatment.

'You let no one in without a ticket,' said Sister Malone to Sister Latch, 'and you treat no one unless the ticket bears today's date and the doctor's signature. You can let the first two in.'

Sister Latch went eagerly. There was already a crowd and it pressed round the door, a collection of dark faces, clothes and rags and nakedness and smells. Sister Latch held up two fingers and cried, 'Two,' in her new Bengali, but seven edged past her into the room.

'It's all right,' said Sister Shelley in her even, toneless voice. 'There are only two. The others are relations,' and she set to work.

The first case was nothing remarkable, a septic ear; a woman of the sweeper class sat herself down on a stool and, clasping her ankles until she was bent almost double, inclined her head to her shoulder so that Sister Shelley could conveniently clean her ear. Sister Malone was poulticing, in a woman's armpit, an abscess which had been opened the day before.

The next two patients came, and then another, an old woman. 'You can attend to her,' said Sister Shelley to Sister Latch. 'She is an old case and knows what to do.' Sister Latch went slowly up to the woman. She was a crone, wound in a meagre grey-white cotton sari that showed her naked waist and withered filthy breasts; her head was shaved and her feet were bare. She sat down on a stool and began to unwind an enormous, dirty bandage on her thumb.

'Don't do that,' said Sister Latch. 'Let me.'

'*Nahin*, baba,' said the old woman, unwinding steadily, 'you fetch the bowl for it to soak in.'

Sister Latch had not been called 'child' before. A little piqued, she looked round. 'That is the bowl,' said the old woman, pointing to a kidney-dish on the table. 'The hot water is there, and there is the medicine.' She had come to the last of the bandage and she shut her eyes. 'You can pull it off,' she said. 'It makes me sick.'

Sister Latch pulled, and a tremor shook her that seemed to open a fissure from her knees through her stomach to her heart. The thumb was a stump, swollen, gangrened. 'It—it makes me sick, too,' said poor Sister Latch, and ran out.

When she came back the thumb was soaking and Sister Shelley was preparing the dressing. 'She is a maidservant in a rich house,' said Sister Shelley without emotion 'and they make her go on working, scouring cooking-pots and washing up; with the thumb continually in water, of course it cannot heal.'

Sister Latch was dumb with indignation and pity.

At that moment Sister Malone came bustling back. 'Ah, Tarala!' she said to the old woman in Bengali. 'Well, how's your disgraceful thumb?' She took it gently from the back. 'Ah, it's better!' She examined it. 'It *is* better. It actually is. Look, Sisters, do you see how it's beginning to slough off here? Isn't that wonderful? Give me the scissors. Now the dressing, Sister, quickly.' Her fingers wound on the bandage swiftly and steadily. She finished and lifted the hand and put it in the bosom of the sari. 'There, that's beautiful,' she said, and the old woman crept out, still seared with pain but comforted.

'But *how* can it heal?' asked Sister Latch, with tears in her sympathetic eyes. 'What is the use?'

'We must hope for the best,' said Sister Malone.

Sister Shelley was silent.

'We must temper our work with faith,' said Sister Malone, emptying the kidney-dish. Steeped in ritual and reality, Sister Malone's words were often accidentally beautiful. 'We must have faith for them, Sister Latch, dear. Sister Shelley, this child is for operation.' She put a piece of brown paper under the child's dusty feet as he lay on the table. He began to scream as Sister Shelley took his hands.

The abscess on his forehead was like a rhinoceros horn; he was a dark little boy, and the skin round the abscess was stretched and strained with colours of olive-green and fig-purple. His eyes rolled with fright, showing the whites, and the muscles of his stomach were drawn in and tensed into the shape of a cave under his ribs. He screamed in short, shrill screams as the doctor came in.

Suddenly Sister Shelley began to scream as well. She was holding the boy's hands out of the way while Sister Malone cleaned his forehead, and now she beat them on the table. 'Stop that noise!' she shrieked. 'Stop that! Stop! Stop that noise!'

Sister Malone knocked her hands away, spun her round by the shoulders and marched her outside, then came in quickly and shut the doors. 'Take her place, Sister Latch,' she said curtly. 'The doctor is here.'

'But—no anaesthetic?' asked Sister Latch.

'There's no money for anaesthetics for a small thing like this,' said Sister Malone sadly. 'Never mind,' she added firmly. 'It is over in a minute.'

The morning went on growing steadily hotter, the smells steadily stronger, the light more blindingly white. The heat in the treatment room was intense, and both sisters were wet, their hands clammy. In half an hour Sister Shelley, made curiously empty and blank by her tears, came back. Sister Malone said nothing. The patients came in until Sister Latch lost count of them; the wounds, the sores, disease and shame were shown; the room echoed with cries, screams, tears—rivers of tears, thought Sister Latch.

Then, in the middle of the hubbub, quiet descended.

A car had driven up, a large car, and from it two young men had jumped down, calling for a stretcher. They were well-dressed young Hindus in white, and between them they lifted from the car something small and fragile and very still, wrapped in vivid violet and green. Sister Latch saw a fall of long black hair.

The stretcher was brought straight into the treatment room, and the girl was lifted from it to the table. She lay inert, with the brilliant colours heaped around her. Her face was a pale oval turned up to the ceiling, her mouth white-brown, her nostrils wide as if they were stamped with fright, and her eyes open, glazed, the pupils enormous. Her hair hung to the floor and she was very young. 'Seventeen?' asked Sister Latch. 'Or sixteen? How beautiful she is.' She looked again and cried, 'Sister, she's dead.'

'She is breathing,' said Sister Malone. Her flat little hand was spread on the girl's heart.

One of the young men was terribly unnerved. Sister Latch wondered if he were the husband. He shivered as he stood waiting by the table. 'She t-took her l-life,' he said.

The other man, darker, stronger, said sternly, 'Be quiet.'

'And why? Why?' asked Sister Malone's eyes, but she said evenly, 'Well, she didn't succeed. She is breathing.'

'You th-think th-there is—hope?'

'There is always hope', said Sister Malone, 'while there is breath.'

Then the doctor and orderlies came in with pails and the stomach-pump and the young men were sent out of the room. Sister Shelley went to the window and stood there with her back to everyone; Sister Malone, after a glance at her, let her stand. 'You will have to help me,' said Sister Malone to Sister Latch. 'Be strong.'

'But—only tell me what it is *about*. I don't understand,' cried Sister Latch, quite out of herself. 'I don't understand.'

'She has poisoned herself,' said Sister Malone. 'Opium poisoning. Look at her eyes.'

'But why?' cried Sister Latch again. 'Why? She's so young. So beautiful. Why should she?'

'It—is best not to be too curious.'

'Yes,' said Sister Shelley suddenly, still with her back to them, 'don't ask. Don't understand. Only try and drag her back—for more.'

After a time the doctor paused; bent; waited another minute; stood up and slowly, still carefully, began to withdraw the tube.

'No!' said Sister Malone, her hands still busy.

'Yes,' said the doctor, and the last of the hideous tube came from the girl's mouth. He wiped her chin, gently closed her mouth and drew down the lids, but the mouth would not stay closed; it dropped open in an O that looked childish and dismayed, contradicting the sternness of the face and sealed lids.

'Snuffed out,' said Sister Malone, as she stood up, gently put the draperies back and looked down on the girl's shut face. 'They have nothing to sustain them,' said Sister Malone, 'nothing at all.'

Sister Latch began to cry quietly. The young men came in and carried the girl away and, from the window, the sisters saw the car drive away, with a last sight of violet and green on the back seat. A tear slid down Sister Latch's cheek. 'Forgive me,' she said but no one answered; her tears slid unnoticed into that great river of tears. 'Forgive me,' said Sister Latch, 'she wore... exactly the same green... as those little parrots.'

She stood in tears; Sister Shelley seemed chiselled in stone, but Sister Malone was tidying up the room for the next patients. 'Nothing to sustain them,' said Sister Malone and sighed.

At the very end of the morning, when they had finished and taken off their aprons, an old man came into the waiting-hall from the doctor's room. He moved slowly and led a small girl by the wrist; he held his ticket uncertainly between his finger and thumb as if he did not know what to do with it.

'Another!' said Sister Shelley. 'It's too late.'

'No,' said Sister Malone with her faithful exactness. 'It wants one minute to one o'clock, when we would stop,' and she took the paper. 'It is nothing,' she said, 'only stitches to be taken out of a cut on the child's lip. I remember her now. You may go, Sisters. It won't take me five minutes.'

Sister Malone was left with the man and the child.

As she lifted the scissors from the steriliser with the forceps she caught his gaze fixed on her and she saw that he was not old, only emaciated until his flesh had sunken in. His skin was a curious dead grey-brown.

'You are ill,' said Sister Malone.

'I am ill,' the man agreed, his voice calm.

Sister Malone turned the little girl to the light. The child began to whimper and the man to plead with her in a voice quite different from the one he had used when he

72

had spoken of himself. 'She will not hurt you. *Nahin. Nahin. Nahin.*'

'Of course I will not hurt you if you stand still,' said Sister Malone to the child. 'Hold her shoulders.'

The child gave two cries as the stitches came out, but she did not move, though the tears ran from her eyes and the sweat poured off the man. When it was over and he could release his hands he staggered. Sister Malone thought he would have fallen if she had not caught him and helped him to a stool. His arm was burning.

'You have fever,' said Sister Malone.

'I continually have fever,' said the man.

'What is it you have?'

'God knows,' he answered but as if he were satisfied, not wondering.

'You don't know? But you are very ill. Haven't you seen the doctor?'

'No.'

'Then you must come with me at once,' said Sister Malone energetically. 'I will take you to the doctor.'

'I do not need a doctor.'

'But—how can we know what to do for you? How can you know?'

'I do not need to know.'

'But you should have medicine—treatment.'

He smiled. 'I have my medicine.'

His smile was so peculiarly calm that it made Sister Malone pause. She looked at him silently, searchingly. He smiled again and opened the front of his shirt and showed her where, round his neck, hung a silver charm on a red thread of the sort she saw every day and all day long round the necks of men and women and children.

He held it and turned his face upwards, and his eyes. 'My medicine,' he said. 'God.'

Sister Malone suddenly flushed. 'That is absurd,' she said. 'You will die.'

'If I die I am happy.'

'But, man!' cried Sister Malone. 'You mean you will give yourself up without a struggle?'

'Why should I struggle?'

'Come with me to the doctor.'

'No.'

'That's sheer senseless obstinacy,' cried Sister Malone. 'If you won't come, let me fetch him to you.'

'No.'

'Obstinate! Obstinate!' Her eyes behind her glasses looked bewildered and even more blind. 'You came for the child,' she said, 'then why not for yourself?'

'She is too young to choose her path. I have chosen.' There was a silence. 'Come Jaya,' he said gently, 'greet the Sister Sahib and we shall go.'

'Wait. Wait one minute. If you won't listen to me, let the doctor talk to you. He is wise and good. Let him talk to you.'

She had barred his way and the man seemed to grow more dignified and a little stern. 'Let me go,' he said. 'I have told you. I need nothing. I have everything. I have God.'

Sister Malone, left alone, was furious as she washed her hands; her face was red and her glasses glittered. 'Mumbo-jumbo!' she said furiously as she turned the tap off. 'Mumbo-jumbo! Heavens! What an obstinate man!'

The Forks

J. F. POWERS

*T*hat summer when Father Eudex got back from saying Mass at the orphanage in the morning, he would park Monsignor's car, which was long and black and new like a politician's, and sit down in the cool of the porch to read his office. If Monsignor was not already standing at the door, he would immediately appear there, seeing that his car had safely returned, and inquire:

'Did you have any trouble with her?'

Father Eudex knew too well the question meant, Did you mistreat my car?

'No trouble, Monsignor.'

'Good,' Monsignor said, with imperfect faith in his curate, who was not a car owner. For a moment Monsignor stood framed in the screen door, fumbling his watch fob as for a full-length portrait, and then he was suddenly not there.

'Monsignor,' Father Eudex said, rising nervously, 'I've got a chance to pick up a car.'

At the door Monsignor slid into his frame again. His face expressed what was for him intense interest.

'Yes? Go on.'

'I don't want to have to use yours every morning.'

'It's all right.'

'And there are other times.' Father Eudex decided not to be maudlin and mention sick calls, nor be entirely honest and admit he was tired of buses and bumming rides from parishioners. 'And now I've got a chance to get one—cheap.'

Monsignor, smiling, came alert at *cheap*.

'New?'

'No, I wouldn't say it's new.'

Monsignor was openly suspicious now. 'What kind?'

'It's a Ford.'

'And not new?'

'Not new, Monsignor—but in good condition. It was owned by a retired farmer and had good care.'

Monsignor sniffed. He *knew* cars. 'V-Eight, Father?'

'No,' Father Eudex confessed. 'It's a Model A.'

Monsignor chuckled as though this were indeed the damnedest thing he had ever heard.

'But in very good condition, Monsignor.'

'You said that.'

'Yes. And I could take it apart if anything went wrong. My uncle had one.'

'No doubt.' Monsignor uttered a laugh at Father Eudex's rural origins. Then he delivered the final word, long delayed out of amusement. 'It wouldn't be prudent, Father. After all, this isn't a country parish. You know the class of people we get here.'

Monsignor put on his Panama hat. Then, apparently mistaking the obstinacy in his curate's face for plain ignorance, he shed a little more light. 'People watch a priest, Father. *Damnant quod non intelligunt*. It would never do. You'll have to watch your tendencies.'

Monsignor's eyes tripped and fell hard on the morning paper lying on the swing where he had finished it.

'Another flattering piece about that crazy fellow... There's a man who might have gone places if it weren't for his mouth! A bishop doesn't have to get mixed up in all that stuff!'

Monsignor, as Father Eudex knew, meant unions, strikes, race riots—all that stuff.

'A parishioner was saying to me only yesterday it's getting so you can't tell the Catholics from the Communists, with the priests as bad as any. Yes, and this fellow is the worst. He reminds me of that bishop a few years back—at least he called himself a bishop, a Protestant— that was advocating companionate marriages. It's not that bad, maybe, but if you listened to some of them you'd think that Catholicity and capitalism were incompatible!'

'The Holy Father—'

'The Holy Father's in Europe, Father. Mr Memmers lives in this parish. I'm his priest. What can I tell him?'

'Is it Mr Memmers of the First National, Monsignor?'

'It is, Father. And there's damned little cheer I can give a man like Memmers. Catholics, priests, and laity alike— yes, and princes of the Church, all talking atheistic communism!'

This was the substance of their conversation, always, the deadly routine in which Father Eudex played straight man. Each time it happened he seemed to participate, and though he should have known better he justified his participation by hoping that it would not happen again, or in quite the same way. But it did, it always did, the same way, and Monsignor, for all his alarums, had nothing to say really and meant one thing only, the thing he never said—that he dearly wanted to be, and was not, a bishop.

Father Eudex could imagine just what kind of bishop Monsignor would be. His reign would be a wise one, excessively so. His mind was made up on everything, excessively so. He would know how to avoid the snares set in the path of the just man, avoid them, too, in good taste and good conscience. He would not be trapped as so many good shepherds before him had been trapped, poor souls—caught in fair-seeming dilemmas of justice that were best left alone, like the first apple. It grieved him, he said, to think of those great hearts broken in silence and solitude. It was the worst kind of exile, alas! But just give him the chance and he would know what to do, what to say, and more important, what not to do, not to say—neither yea nor nay for him. He had not gone to Rome for nothing. For him the dark forest of decisions would not exist; for him, thanks to hours spent in prayer and meditation, the forest would vanish as dry grass before fire, his fire. He knew the mask of evil already—birth control, indecent movies, salacious books—and would call these things by their right names and dare to deal with them for what they were, these new occasions for the old sins of the cities of the plains.

But in the meantime—oh, to have a particle of the faith that God had in humanity! Dear, trusting God forever trying them beyond their feeble powers, ordering terrible tests, fatal trials by nonsense (the crazy bishop). And keeping Monsignor steadily warming up on the side lines, ready to rush in, primed for the day that would perhaps never dawn.

At one time, so the talk went, there had been reason to

think that Monsignor was headed for a bishopric. Now it was too late; Monsignor's intercessors were all dead; the cupboard was bare; he knew it at heart, and it galled him to see another man, this *crazy* man, given the opportunity, and making such a mess of it.

Father Eudex searched for and found a little salt for Monsignor's wound. 'The word's going around he'll be the next archbishop,' he said.

'I won't believe it,' Monsignor countered hoarsely. He glanced at the newspaper on the swing and renewed his horror. 'If that fellow's right, Father, I'm'—his voice cracked at the idea—'*wrong!*'

Father Eudex waited until Monsignor had started down the steps to the car before he said, 'It could be.'

'I'll be back for lunch, Father. I'm taking her for a little spin.'

Monsignor stopped in admiration a few feet from the car—her. He was as helpless before her beauty as a boy with a birthday bicycle. He could not leave her alone. He had her out every morning and afternoon and evening. He was indiscriminate about picking people up for a ride in her. He kept her on a special diet—only the best of gas and oil and grease, with daily rubdowns. He would run her only on the smoothest roads and at so many miles an hour. That was to have stopped at the first five hundred, but only now, nearing the thousand mark, was he able to bring himself to increase her speed, and it seemed to hurt him more than it did her.

Now he was walking around behind her to inspect the tyres. Apparently O.K. He gave the left rear fender an amorous chuck and eased into the front seat. Then they drove off, the car and he, to see the world, to explore each other further on the honeymoon.

Father Eudex watched the car slide into the traffic, and waited, on edge. The corner cop, fulfilling Father Eudex's fears, blew his whistle and waved his arms up in all four directions, bringing traffic to a standstill. Monsignor pulled expertly out of line and drove down Clover Boulevard in a one-car parade; all others stalled respectfully. The cop, as Monsignor passed, tipped his cap, showing a bald head. Monsignor, in the circumstances, could not acknowledge him, though he knew the man well—a parishioner. He was occupied with keeping his countenance kindly, grim, and exalted, that the cop's faith remain whole, for it was evidently inconceivable to him that Monsignor should ever venture abroad unless to bear the Holy Viaticum, always racing with death.

Father Eudex, eyes baleful but following the progress of the big black car, saw a hand dart out of the driver's window in a wave. Monsignor would combine a lot of business with pleasure that morning, creating what he called 'good will for the Church'—all morning in the driver's seat toasting passers-by with a wave that was better than a blessing. How he loved waving to people!

Father Eudex overcame his inclination to sit and stew about things by going down the steps to meet the mailman. He got the usual handful for the Monsignor—advertisements and amazing offers, the unfailing crop of chaff from dealers in church goods, organs, collection schemes, insurance, and sacramental wines. There were two envelopes addressed to Father Eudex, one a mimeographed plea from a missionary society which he might or might not acknowledge with a contribution, depending upon what he thought of the cause—if it was really lost enough to justify a levy on his poverty—and the other a cheque for a hundred dollars.

The cheque came in an eggshell envelope with no explanation except a tiny card, 'Compliments of the Rival Tractor Company,' but even that was needless. All over town clergymen had known for days that the cheques were on the way again. Some, rejoicing, could hardly wait. Father Eudex, however, was one of those who could.

With the passing of hard times and the coming of the fruitful war years, the Rival Company, which was a great one for public relations, had found the best solution to the excess-profits problem to be giving. Ministers and even rabbis shared in the annual jack pot, but Rival employees were largely Catholic and it was the cheques to the priests that paid off. Again, some thought it was a wonderful idea, and others thought that Rival, plagued by strikes and justly so, had put their alms to work.

There was another eggshell envelope, Father Eudex saw, among the letters for Monsignor, and knew his cheque would be for two hundred, the premium for pastors.

Father Eudex left Monsignor's mail on the porch table by his cigars. His own he stuck in the back pocket, wanting to forget it, and went down the steps into the yard. Walking back and forth on the shady side of the rectory where the lilies of the valley grew and reading his office, he gradually drifted into the back yard, lured by a noise. He came upon Whalen, the janitor, pounding pegs into the ground.

Father Eudex closed the breviary on a finger. 'What's it all about Joe?'

Joe Whalen snatched a piece of paper from his shirt and handed it to Father Eudex. 'He gave it to me this morning.'

He—it was the word for Monsignor among them. A docile pronoun only, and yet when it meant the Monsignor it said, and concealed, nameless things.

The paper was a plan for a garden drawn up by the Monsignor in his fine hand. It called for a huge fleur-de-lis bounded by smaller crosses—and these Maltese—a fountain, a sundial, and a cloister walk running from the rectory to the garage. Later there would be birdhouses and a ten-foot wall of thick grey stones, acting as a moat against the eyes of the world. The whole scheme struck Father Eudex as expensive and, in this country, Presbyterian.

When Monsignor drew the plan, however, he must have been in his medieval mood. A spouting whale jostled with Neptune in the choppy waters of the fountain. North was indicated in the legend by a winged cherub huffing and puffing.

Father Eudex held the plan up against the sun to see the watermark. The stationery was new to him, heavy, simulated parchment, with the Church of the Holy Redeemer and Monsignor's name embossed, three initials, W. F. X., William Francis Xavier. With all those initials the man could pass for a radio station, a chancery wit had observed, or if his last name had not been Sweeney, Father Eudex added now, for high Anglican.

Father Eudex returned the plan to Whalen, feeling sorry for him and to an extent guilty before him—if only because he was a priest like Monsignor (now turned architect) whose dream of a monastery garden included the over-worked janitor under the head of 'labour.'

Father Eudex asked Whalen to bring another shovel. Together, almost without words, they worked all morning spading up crosses, leaving the big fleur-de-lis to the last.

Father Eudex removed his coat first, then his collar, and finally was down to his undershirt.

Towards noon Monsignor rolled into the driveway.

He stayed in the car, getting red in the face, recovering from the pleasure of seeing so much accomplished as he slowly recognized his curate in Whalen's helper. In a still, appalled voice he called across the lawn, 'Father,' and waited as for a beast that might or might not have sense enough to come.

Father Eudex dropped his shovel and went over to the car, shirtless.

Monsignor waited a moment before he spoke, as though annoyed by the everlasting necessity, where this person was concerned, to explain. 'Father,' he said quietly at last, 'I wouldn't do any more of that—if I were you. Rather, in any event, I wouldn't.'

'All right, Monsignor.'

'To say the least, it's not prudent. If necessary'—he paused as Whalen came over to dig a cross within ear-shot—'I'll explain later. It's time for lunch now.'

The car, black, beautiful, fierce with chromium, was quiet as Monsignor dismounted, knowing her master. Monsignor went around to the rear, felt a tyre, and probed a nasty cinder in the tread.

'Look at that,' he said, removing the cinder.

Father Eudex thought he saw the car lift a hoof, gaze around, and thank Monsignor with her headlights.

Monsignor proceeded at a precise pace to the back door of the rectory. There he held the screen open momentarily, as if remembering something or reluctant to enter before himself—such was his humility—but then called to Whalen with an intimacy that could never exist between them.

83

'Better knock off now, Joe.'

Whalen turned in on himself. *'Joe*—is it!'

Father Eudex removed his clothes from the grass. His hands were all blisters, but in them he found a little absolution. He apologized to Joe for having to take the afternoon off. 'I can't make it, Joe. Something turned up.'

'Sure, Father.'

Father Eudex could hear Joe telling his wife about it that night—yeah, the young one got in wrong with the old one again. Yeah, the old one, he don't believe in it, work, for them.

Father Eudex paused in the kitchen to remember he knew not what. It was in his head, asking to be let in, but he did not place it until he heard Monsignor in the next room complaining about the salad to the housekeeper. It was the voice of dear, dead Aunt Hazel, coming from the summer he was ten. He translated the past into the present: I can't come out and play this afternoon, Joe, on account of my monsignor won't let me.

In the dining room Father Eudex sat down at the table and said grace. He helped himself to a chop, creamed new potatoes, pickled beets, jelly, and bread. He liked jelly. Monsignor passed the butter.

'That's supposed to be a tutti-frutti salad,' Monsignor said, grimacing at his. 'But she used green olives.'

Father Eudex said nothing.

'I said she used green olives.'

'I like green olives all right.'

'*I* like green olives, but *not* in tutti-frutti salad.'

Father Eudex replied by eating a green olive, but he knew it could not end there.

'Father,' Monsignor said in a new tone. 'How would you like to go away and study for a year?'

'Don't think I'd care for it, Monsignor. I'm not the type.'

'You're no canonist, you mean?'

'That's one thing.'

'Yes. Well, there are other things it might not hurt you to know. To be quite frank with you, Father, I think you need broadening.'

'I guess so,' Father Eudex said thickly.

'And still, with your tendencies... and with the universities honeycombed with Communists. No, that would never do. I think I meant seasoning, not broadening.'

'Oh.'

'No offence?'

'No offence.'

Who would have thought a little thing like an olive could lead to all this, Father Eudex mused—who but himself, that is, for his association with Monsignor had shown him that anything could lead to everything. Monsignor was a master at making points. Nothing had changed since the day Father Eudex walked into the rectory saying he was the new assistant. Monsignor had evaded Father Eudex's hand in greeting, and a few days later, after he began to get the range, he delivered a lecture on the whole subject of handshaking. It was Middle West to shake hands, or South West, or West in any case, and it was not done where he came from, and— why had he ever come from where he came from? Not to be reduced to shaking hands, you could bet! Handshaking was worse than foot washing and unlike the pious practice there was nothing to support it. And from handshaking Monsignor might go into a general discussion of Father Eudex's failings. He used the open forum method, but he was the only speaker and there was never time enough for questions from the audience. Monsignor seized his examples at random from life. He saw Father Eudex coming out of his bedroom in pyjama bottoms only and so told him about the dressing gown, its purpose, something of its history. He advised Father Eudex to barber his armpits, for it was being done all over now. He let Father Eudex see his bottle of cologne, 'Steeple,' special for clergymen, and said he should not be afraid of it. He suggested that Father Eudex shave his face oftener, too. He loaned him his Rogers Peet catalogue, which had sketches of clerical blades togged out in the latest, and prayed that he would stop going around looking like a rabbinical student.

He found Father Eudex reading *The Catholic Worker* one day and had not trusted him since. Father Eudex's conception of the priesthood was evangelical in the worst sense, barbaric, gross, foreign to the mind of the Church, which was one of two terms he used as sticks to beat him with. The other was taste. The air of the rectory was often heavy with The Mind of the Church and Taste.

Another thing. Father Eudex could not conduct a civil conversation. Monsignor doubted that Father Eudex could even think to himself with anything like agreement. Certainly any discussion with Father Eudex ended inevitably in argument or sighing. Sighing! Why didn't people talk up if they had anything to say? No, they'd rather sigh! Father, don't ever, ever sigh at me again!

Finally, Monsignor did not like Father Eudex's table manners. This came to a head one night when Monsignor, seeing his curate's plate empty and all the silverware at his place unused except for a single knife, fork, and spoon, exploded altogether, saying it had been on his

mind for weeks, and then descending into the vernacular
he declared that Father Eudex did not know the forks—
now perhaps he could understand that! Meals, unless
Monsignor had guests or other things to struggle with,
were always occasions of instruction for Father Eudex,
and sometimes of chastisement.

And now he knew the worst—if Monsignor was
thinking of recommending him for a year of study, in a
Sulpician seminary probably, to learn the forks. So this
was what it meant to be a priest. *Come, follow me, Going
forth, teach ye all nations. Heal the sick, raise the dead, cleanse
the lepers, cast out devils.* Teach the class of people we get
here? Teach Mr Memmers? Teach Communists? Teach
Monsignors? And where were the poor? The lepers of
old? The lepers were in their colonies with nuns to nurse
them. The poor were in their holes and would not come
out. Mr Memmers was in his bank, without cheer. The
Communists were in their universities, awaiting a sign.
And he was at table with Monsignor, and it was enough
for the disciple to be as his master, but the housekeeper
had used green olives.

Monsignor inquired, 'Did you get your cheque today?'

Father Eudex looked up, considered. 'I got *a* cheque,'
he said.

'From the Rival people, I mean?'

'Yes.'

'Good. Well, I think you might apply it on the car
you're wanting. A decent car. That's a worthy cause.'
Monsignor noticed that he was not taking it well. 'Not
that I mean to dictate what you shall do with your little
windfall, Father. It's just that I don't like to see you
mortifying yourself with a Model A—and disgracing the
Church.'

'Yes,' Father Eudex said, suffering.

'Yes. I dare say you don't see the danger, just as you didn't a while ago when I found you making a spectacle of yourself with Whalen. You just don't see the danger because you just don't think. Not to dwell on it, but I seem to remember some overshoes.'

The overshoes! Monsignor referred to them as to the Fall. Last winter Father Eudex had given his overshoes to a freezing picket. It had got back to Monsignor and—good Lord, a man could have his sympathies, but he had no right clad in the cloth to endanger the prestige of the Church by siding in these wretched squabbles. Monsignor said he hated to think of all the evil done by people doing good! Had Father Eudex ever heard of the Albigensian heresy, or didn't the seminary teach that any more?

Father Eudex declined dessert. It was strawberry mousse.

'Delicious,' Monsignor said. 'I think I'll let her stay.'

At that moment Father Eudex decided that he had nothing to lose. He placed his knife next to his fork on the plate, adjusted them his way and that until they seemed to work a combination in his mind, to spring a lock which in turn enabled him to speak out.

'Monsignor,' he said. 'I think I ought to tell you I don't intend to make use of that money. In fact—to show you how my mind works—I have even considered endorsing the cheque to the strikers' relief fund.'

'So,' Monsignor said calmly—years in the confessional had prepared him for anything.

'I'll admit I don't know whether I can in justice. And even if I could I don't know that I would. I don't know why... I guess hush money, no matter what you do with it, is lousy.'

Monsignor regarded him with piercing baby blue eyes. 'You'd find it pretty hard to prove, Father, that *any* money *in se* is... what you say it is. I would quarrel further with the definition "hush money " It seems to me nothing if not rash that you would presume to impugn the motive of the Rival Company in sending out those cheques. You would seem to challenge the whole concept of good works—not that I am ignorant of the misuses to which money can be put.' Monsignor, changing tack, tucked it all into a sigh. 'Perhaps I'm just a simple soul, and it's enough for me to know personally some of the people in the Rival company and to know them good people. Many of them Catholic...' A throb had crept into Monsignor's voice. He shut it off.

'I don't mean anything that subtle, Monsignor,' Father Eudex said. 'I'm just telling you, as my pastor, what I'm going to do with the cheque. Or what I'm not going to do with it. I don't know what I'm going to do with it. Maybe send it back.'

Monsignor rose from the table, slightly smiling. 'Very well, Father. But there's always the poor.'

Monsignor took leave of Father Eudex with a laugh. Father Eudex felt it was supposed to fool him into thinking that nothing he had said would be used against him. It showed, rather, that Monsignor was not winded, that he had broken wild curates before, plenty of them, and that he would ride again.

Father Eudex sought the shade of the porch. He tried to read his office, but was drowsy. He got up for a glass of water. The saints in Ireland used to stand up to their necks in cold water, but not for drowsiness. When he came back to the porch a woman was ringing the doorbell. She looked like a customer for rosary beads.

'Hello,' he said.

'I'm Mrs Klein, Father, and I was wondering if you could help me out.'

Father Eudex straightened a porch chair for her. 'Please sit down.'

'It's a German name, Father. Klein was German descent,' she said, and added with a silly grin, 'It ain't what you think, Father.'

'I beg your pardon.'

'Klein. Some think it's a Jew name. But they stole it from Klein.'

Father Eudex decided to come back to that later. 'You were wondering if I could help you?'

'Yes, Father. It's personal.'

'Is it matter for confession?'

'Oh no, Father.' He had made her blush.

'Then go ahead.'

Mrs Klein peered into the honeysuckle vines on either side of the porch for alien ears.

'No one can hear you, Mrs Klein.'

'Father—I'm just a poor widow,' she said, and continued as though Father Eudex had just slandered the man. 'Klein was awful good to me, Father.'

'I'm sure he was.'

'So good... and he went and left me all he had.' She had begun to cry a little.

Father Eudex nodded gently. She was after something, probably not money, always the best bet—either that or a drunk in the family—but this one was not Irish. Perhaps just sympathy.

'I come to get your advice, Father. Klein always said, "If you got a problem, Freda, see the priest." '

'Do you need money?'

'I got more than I can use from the bakery.'

'You have a bakery?'

Mrs Klein nodded down the street. 'That's my bakery. It was Klein's. The Purity.'

'I go by there all the time,' Father Eudex said, abandoning himself to her. He must stop trying to shape the conversation and let her work it out.

'Will you give me your advice, Father?' He felt that she sensed his indifference and interpreted it as his way of rejecting her. She either had no idea how little sense she made or else supreme faith in him, as a priest, to see into her heart.

'Just what is it you're after, Mrs Klein?'

'He left me all he had, Father, but it's just laying in the bank.'

'And you want me to tell you what to do with it?'

'Yes, Father.'

Father Eudex thought this might be interesting, certainly a change. He went back in his mind to the seminary and the class in which they had considered the problem of inheritances. Do we have any unfulfilled obligations? Are we sure?... Are there any impedimenta?

'Do you have any dependents, Mrs Klein—any children?'

'One boy, Father. I got him running the bakery. I pay him good—too much, Father.'

'Is "too much" a living wage?'

'Yes, Father. He ain't got a family.'

'A living wage is not too much,' Father Eudex handed down, sailing into the encyclical style without knowing it.

Mrs. Klein was smiling over having done something good without knowing precisely what it was.

'How old is your son?'

'He's thirty-six Father.'

'Not married?'

'No, Father, but he's got him a girl.' She giggled, and Father Eudex, embarrassed, retied his shoe.

'But you don't care to make a will and leave this money to your son in the usual way?'

'I guess I'll have to... if I die.' Mrs. Klein was suddenly crushed and haunted, but whether by death or charity, Father Eudex did not know.

'You don't have to, Mrs Klein. There are many worthy causes. And the worthiest is the cause of the poor. My advice to you, if I understand your problem, is to give what you have to someone who needs it.'

Mrs Klein just stared at him.

'You could even leave it to the archdiocese,' he said, completing the sentence to himself: but I don't recommend it in your case... with your tendencies. You look like an Indian giver to me.

But Mrs Klein had got enough, 'Huh!' she said, rising. 'Well! You *are* a funny one!'

And then Father Eudex realized that she had come to him for a broker's tip. It was in the eyes. The hat. The dress. The shoes. 'If you'd like to speak to the pastor,' he said, 'come back in the evening.'

'You're a nice young man,' Mrs Klein said, rather bitter now and bent on getting away from him. 'But I got to say this—you ain't much of a priest. And Klein said if I got a problem, see the priest—huh! You ain't much of a priest! What time's your boss come in?'

'In the evening,' Father Eudex said. 'Come any time in the evening.'

Mrs Klein was already down the steps and making for the street.

'You might try Mr Memmers at the First National,'
Father Eudex called, actually trying to help her, but she
must have thought it was just some more of his nonsense
and did not reply.

After Mrs Klein had disappeared Father Eudex went to
his room. In the hallway upstairs Monsignor's voice,
coming from the depths of the clerical nap, halted him.

'Who was it?'

'A woman,' Father Eudex said. 'A woman seeking
good counsel.'

He waited a moment to be questioned, but Monsignor
was not awake enough to see anything wrong with that,
and there came only a sigh and a shifting of weight that
told Father Eudex he was simply turning over in bed.

Father Eudex walked into the bathroom. He took the
Rival cheque from his pocket. He tore it into little
squares. He let them flutter into the toilet. He pulled the
chain hard.

He went to his room and stood looking out the window
at nothing. He could hear the others already giving an
account of their stewardship, but could not judge them. I
bought baseball uniforms for the school. I bought the nuns
a new washing machine. I purchased a Mass kit for a
Chinese missionary. I bought a set of matched irons. Mine
helped pay for keeping my mother in a rest home upstate.
I gave mine to the poor.

And you, Father?

Death in Jerusalem

WILLIAM TREVOR

'*T*ill then,' Father Paul said, leaning out of the train window. 'Till Jerusalem, Francis.'

'Please God, Paul.' As he spoke the Dublin train began to move and his brother waved from the window and he waved back, a modest figure on the platform. Everyone said Francis might have been a priest as well, meaning that Francis's quietness and meditative disposition had an air of the cloister about them. But Francis contented himself with the running of Conary's hardware business, which his mother had run until she was too old for it. 'Are we game for the Holy Land next year?' Father Paul had asked that July. 'Will we go together, Francis?' He had brushed aside all Francis's protestations, all attempts to explain that the shop could not be left, that their mother would be confused by the absence of Francis from the house. Rumbustiously he'd pointed out that there was their sister Kitty, who was in charge of the household of which Francis and their mother were part and whose husband, Myles, could surely be trusted to look after the shop for a single fortnight. For thirty years, ever since he was seven, Francis had wanted to go to the Holy Land. He had savings which he'd never spent a penny of: you couldn't take them with you, Father Paul had more than once stated that July.

On the platform Francis watched until the train could no longer be seen, his thoughts still with his brother. The priest's ruddy countenance smiled again behind cigarette smoke; his bulk remained impressive in his clerical clothes, the collar pinching the flesh of his neck, his black shoes scrupulously polished. There were freckles on the backs of his large, strong hands; he had a fine head of hair, grey and crinkly. In an hour and a half's time the train would creep into Dublin, and he'd take a taxi. He'd spend a night in the Gresham Hotel, probably falling in with another priest, having a drink or two, maybe playing a game of bridge after his meal. That was his brother's way and always had been—an extravagant, easy kind of way, full of smiles and good humour. It was what had taken him to America and made him successful there. In order to raise money for the church that he and Father Steigmuller intended to build before 1980 he took parties of the well-to-do from San Francisco to Rome and Florence, to Chartres and Seville and the Holy Land. He was good at raising money, not just for the church but for the boys' home of which he was president, and for the Hospital of Our Saviour, and for St Mary's Old People's Home on the west side of the city. But every July he flew back to Ireland, to the town in Co. Tipperary where his mother and brother and sister lived. He stayed in the house above the shop which he might have inherited himself on the death of his father, which he'd rejected in favour of the religious life. Mrs Conary was eighty now. In the shop she sat silently behind the counter, in a corner by the chicken-wire, wearing only clothes that were black. In the evenings she sat with Francis in the lace-curtained sitting-room, while the rest of the family occupied the kitchen. It was for her sake most of all that Father Paul made the journey every summer, considering it his duty.

Walking back to the town from the station, Francis was aware that he was missing his brother. Father Paul was fourteen years older and in childhood had often taken the place of their father, who had died when Francis was five. His brother had possessed an envied strength and knowledge; he'd been quite a hero, quite often worshipped, an example of success. In later life he had become an example of generosity as well: ten years ago he'd taken their mother to Rome, and their sister Kitty and her husband two years later; he'd paid the expenses when their sister Edna had gone to Canada; he'd assisted two nephews to make a start in America. In childhood Francis hadn't possessed his brother's healthy freckled face, just as in middle age he didn't have his ruddy complexion and his stoutness and his easiness with people. His breathing was sometimes laboured because of wheeziness in the chest. In the ironmonger's shop he wore a brown cotton coat.

'Hullo, Mr Conary,' a woman said to him in the main street of the town. 'Father Paul's gone off, has he?'

'Yes, he's gone again.'

'I'll pray for his journey so,' the woman promised, and Francis thanked her.

A year went by. In San Francisco another wing of the boys' home was completed, another target was reached in Father Paul and Father Steigmuller's fund for the church they planned to have built by 1980. In the town in Co. Tipperary there were baptisms and burial services and First Communions. Old Loughlin, a farmer from Bansha, died in McSharry's grocery and bar, having gone there to celebrate a good price he'd got for a heifer. Clancy, from behind the counter in Doran's drapery, married Maureen Talbot; Mr Nolan's plasterer married Miss Carron; Johneen Meagher married Seamus in the chipshop, under pressure from her family to do so. A local horse, from the stables on the Limerick road, was said to be an entry for the Fairyhouse Grand National, but it turned out not to be true. Every evening of that year Francis sat with his mother in the lace-curtained sittingroom above the shop. Every weekday she sat in her corner by the chicken-wire, watching while he counted out screws and weighed staples, or advised about yard brushes or tap-washers. Occasionally, on a Saturday, he visited the three Christian Brothers who lodged with Mrs Shea and afterwards he'd tell his mother about how the authority was slipping these days from the nuns and the Christian Brothers, and how Mrs Shea's elderly maid, Ita, couldn't see to cook the food any more. His mother would nod and hardly ever speak. When he told a joke—what young Hogan had said when he'd found a nail in his egg or how Ita had put mint sauce into a jug with milk in it— she never laughed, and looked at him in surprise when he laughed himself. But Dr Foran said it was best to keep her cheered up.

All during that year Francis talked to her about his forthcoming visit to the Holy Land, endeavouring to make her understand that for a fortnight next spring he would be away from the house and the shop. He'd been away before for odd days, but that was when she'd been younger. He used to visit an aunt in Tralee, but three years ago the aunt died and he hadn't left the town since.

Francis and his mother had always been close. Before his birth two daughters had died in infancy, and his very survival had often stuck Mrs Conary as a gift. He had always been her favourite, the one among her children whom she often considered least able to stand on his own two feet. It was just like Paul to have gone blustering off to San Francisco instead of remaining in Co. Tipperary. It was just like Kitty to have married a useless man. 'There's not a girl in the town who'd touch him,' she'd said to her daughter at the time, but Kitty had been headstrong and adamant, and there was Myles now, doing nothing whatsoever except cleaning other people's windows for a pittance and placing bets in Donovan's the turf accountant's. It was the shop and the arrangement Kitty had with Francis and her mother that kept her and the children going, three of whom had already left the town, which in Mrs Conary's opinion they mightn't have done if they'd had a better type of father. Mrs Conary often wondered what her own two babies who'd died might have grown up into, and imagined they might have been like Francis, about whom she'd never had a moment's worry. Not in a million years would he give you the feeling that he was too big for his boots, like Paul sometimes did with his lavishness and his big talk of America. He wasn't silly like Kitty, or so sinful you couldn't forgive him, the way you couldn't forgive Edna, even though she was dead and buried in Toronto.

Francis understood how his mother felt about the family. She'd had a hard life, left a widow early on, trying to do the best she could for everyone. In turn he did his best to compensate for the struggles and disappointments she'd suffered, cheering her in the evenings while Kitty and Myles and the youngest of their children watched the television in the kitchen. His mother had ignored the existence of Myles for ten years, ever since the day he'd taken money out of the till to pick up the odds on Gusty Spirit at Phoenix Park. And although Francis got on well enough with Myles he quite understood that there should be a long aftermath to that day. There'd been a terrible row in the kitchen, Kitty screaming at Myles and Myles telling lies and Francis trying to keep them calm, saying they'd give the old woman a heart attack.

She didn't like upsets of any kind, so all during the year before he was to visit the Holy Land Francis read the New Testament to her in order to prepare her. He talked to her about Bethlehem and Nazareth and the miracle of the loaves and fishes and all the other miracles. She kept nodding, but he often wondered if she didn't assume he was just casually referring to episodes in the Bible. As a child he had listened to such talk himself, with awe and fascination, imagining the walking on the water and the temptation in the wilderness. He had imagined the cross carried to Calvary, and the rock rolled back from the tomb, and the rising from the dead on the third day. That he was now to walk in such places seemed extraordinary to him, and he wished his mother was younger so that she could appreciate his good fortune and share it with him when she received the postcards he intended, every day, to send her. But her eyes seemed always to tell him that he was making a mistake, that somehow he was making a fool of himself by doing such a showy thing as going to the Holy Land. *I have the entire itinerary mapped out*, his brother wrote from San Francisco. *There's nothing we'll miss*.

It was the first time Francis had been in an aeroplane.

He flew by Aer Lingus from Dublin to London and then changed to an El Al flight to Tel Aviv. He was nervous and he found it exhausting. All the time he seemed to be eating, and it was strange being among so many people he didn't know. 'You will taste honey such as never before,' an Israeli businessman in the seat next to his assured him. 'And Galilean figs. Make certain to taste Galilean figs.' Make certain too, the businessman went on, to experience Jerusalem by night and in the early dawn. He urged Francis to see places he had never heard of, Yad Va-Shem, the treasures of the Shrine of the Book. He urged him to honour the martyrs of Masada and to learn a few words of Hebrew as a token of respect. He told him of a shop where he could buy mementoes and warned him against Arab street traders.

'The hard man, how are you?' Father Paul said at Tel Aviv airport, having flown in from San Francisco the day before. Father Paul had had a drink or two and he suggested another when they arrived at the Plaza Hotel in Jerusalem. It was half past nine in the evening. 'A quick little nightcap,' Father Paul insisted, 'and then hop into bed with you, Francis.' They sat in an enormous open lounge with low, round tables and square modern armchairs. Father Paul said it was the bar.

They had said what had to be said in the car from Tel Aviv to Jerusalem. Father Paul had asked about their mother, and Kitty and Myles. He'd asked about other people in the town, Old Canon Mahon and Sergeant Murray. He and Father Steigmuller had had a great year of it, he reported: as well as everything else, the boys' home had turned out two tip-top footballers. 'We'll start on a tour at half-nine in the morning,' he said. 'I'll be sitting having breakfast at eight.'

Francis went to bed and Father Paul ordered another whisky, with ice. To his great disappointment there was no Irish whiskey in the hotel so he'd had to content himself with Haig. He fell into conversation with an American couple, making them promise that if they were ever in Ireland they wouldn't miss out Co. Tipperary. At eleven o'clock the barman said he was wanted at the reception desk and when Father Paul went there and announced himself he was given a message in an envelope. It was a telegram that had come, the girl said in poor English. Then she shook her head, saying it was a telex. He opened the envelope and learnt that Mrs Conary had died.

Francis fell asleep immediately and dreamed that he was a boy again, out fishing with a friend whom he couldn't now identify.

On the telephone Father Paul ordered whisky and ice to be brought to his room. Before drinking it he took his jacket off and knelt by his bed to pray for his mother's salvation. When he'd completed the prayers he walked slowly up and down the length of the room, occasionally sipping at his whisky. He argued with himself and finally arrived at a decision.

For breakfast they had scrambled eggs that looked like yellow ice-cream, and orange juice that was delicious. Francis wondered about bacon, but Father Paul explained that bacon was not readily available in Israel.

'Did you sleep all right?' Father Paul inquired. 'Did you have the jet-lag?'

'Jet-lag?'

'A tiredness you get after jet flights. It'd knock you out for days.'

'Ah, I slept great, Paul.'

'Good man.'

They lingered over breakfast. Father Paul reported a little more of what had happened in his parish during the year, in particular about the two young footballers from the boys' home. Francis told about the decline in the cooking at Mrs Shea's boarding-house, as related to him by the three Christian Brothers. 'I have a car laid on,' Father Paul said, and twenty minutes later they walked out into the Jerusalem sunshine.

The hired car stopped on the way to the walls of the Old City. It drew into a lay-by at Father Paul's request and the two men got out and looked across a wide valley dotted with houses and olive trees. A road curled along the distant slope opposite. 'The Mount of Olives,' Father Paul said. 'And that's the road to Jericho.' He pointed more particularly. 'You see that group of eight big olives? Just off the road, where the church is?'

Francis thought he did, but was not sure. There were so many olive trees, and more than one church. He glanced at his brother's pointing finger and followed its direction with his glance.

'The Garden of Gethsemane,' Father Paul said.

Francis did not say anything. He continued to gaze at the distant church, with the clump of olive trees beside it. Wild flowers were profuse on the slopes of the valley, smears of orange and blue on land that looked poor. Two Arab women herded goats.

'Could we see it closer?' he asked, and his brother said that definitely they would. They returned to the waiting car and Father Paul ordered it to the Gate of St Stephen.

Tourists heavy with cameras thronged the Via Dolorosa. Brown, bare-foot children asked for alms. Stallkeepers pressed their different wares: cotton dresses, metal-ware, mementoes, sacred goods. 'Get out of the way,' Father Paul kept saying to them, genially laughing to show he wasn't being abrupt. Francis wanted to stand still and close his eyes, to visualize for a moment the carrying of the Cross. But the ceremony of the Stations, familiar to him for as long as he could remember, was unreal. Try as he would, Christ's journey refused to enter his imagination, and his own plain church seemed closer to the heart of the matter than the noisy lane he was now being jostled on. 'God damn it, of course it's genuine,' an angry American voice proclaimed, in reply to a shriller voice which insisted that cheating had taken place. The voices argued about a piece of wood, neat beneath plastic in a little box, a sample or not of the Cross that had been carried.

They arrived at the Church of the Holy Sepulchre, and at the Chapel of the Nailing to the Cross, where they prayed. They passed through the Chapel of the Angel, to the tomb of Christ. Nobody spoke in the marble cell, but when they left the church Francis overheard a quiet man with spectacles saying it was unlikely that a body would have been buried within the walls of the city. They walked to Hezekiah's Pool and out of the Old City at the Jaffa Gate, where their hired car was waiting for them. 'Are you peckish?' Father Paul asked, and although Francis said he wasn't they returned to the hotel.

Delay funeral till Monday was the telegram Father Paul had sent. There was an early flight on Sunday, in time for an afternoon one from London to Dublin. With luck there'd be a late train on Sunday evening and if there wasn't they'd have to fix a car. Today was Tuesday. It would give them four and a half days. *Funeral eleven Monday* the telegram at the reception desk now confirmed.

'Ah, isn't that great?' he said to himself, bundling the telegram up.

'Will we have a small one?' he suggested in the open area that was the bar. 'Or better still a big one.' He laughed. He was in good spirits in spite of the death that had taken place. He gestured at the barman, wagging his head and smiling jovially.

His face had reddened in the morning sun; there were specks of sweat on his forehead and his nose. 'Bethlehem this afternoon,' he laid down. 'Unless the jet-lag...?'

'I haven't got the jet-lag.'

In the Nativity Boutique Francis brought for his mother a small metal plate with a fish on it. He had stood for a moment, scarcely able to believe it, on the spot where the manger had been, in the Church of the Nativity. As in the Via Dolorosa it had been difficult to clear his mind of the surroundings that now were present: the exotic Greek Orthodox trappings, the foreign-looking priests, the oriental smell. Gold, frankincense and myrrh, he'd kept thinking, for somehow the church seemed more the church of the kings than of Joseph and Mary and their child. Afterwards they returned to Jerusalem, to the Tomb of the Virgin and the Garden of Gethsemane. 'It could have been anywhere,' he heard the quiet, bespectacled sceptic remarking in Gethsemane. 'They're only guessing.'

Father Paul rested in the late afternoon, lying down on his bed with his jacket off. He slept from half past five until a quarter past seven and awoke refreshed. He picked up the telephone and asked for a whisky and ice to be brought up and when it arrived he undressed and had a bath, relaxing in the warm water with the drink on a ledge in the tiled wall beside him.

There would be time to take in Nazareth and Galilee. He was particularly keen that his brother should see Galilee because Galilee had atmosphere and was beautiful. There wasn't, in his own opinion, very much to Nazareth but it would be a pity to miss it all the same. It was at the Sea of Galilee that he intended to tell his brother of their mother's death.

We've had a great day, Francis wrote on a postcard that showed an aerial view of Jerusalem. *The Church of the Holy Sepulchre, where Our Lord's tomb is, and Gethsemane and Bethlehem. Paul's in great form.* He addressed it to his mother, and then wrote other cards, to Kitty and Myles and to the three Christian Brothers in Mrs Shea's, and to Canon Mahon. He gave thanks that he was privileged to be in Jerusalem. He read St Mark and some of St Matthew. He said his rosary.

'Will we chance the wine?' Father Paul said at dinner, not that wine was something he went in for, but a waiter had come up and put a large padded wine-list into his hand.

'Ah, no, no,' Francis protested, but already Father Paul was running his eye down the listed bottles.

'Have you local wine?' he inquired of the waiter. 'A nice red one?'

The waiter nodded and hurried away, and Francis hoped he wouldn't get drunk, the red wine on top of the whisky he'd had in the bar before the meal. He'd only had the one whisky, not being much used to it, making it last through his brother's three.

'I heard some gurriers in the bar,' Father Paul said, 'making a great song and dance about the local red wine.'

Wine made Francis think of the Holy Communion, but he didn't say so. He said the soup was delicious and he drew his brother's attention to the custom there was in the hotel of a porter ringing a bell and walking about with a person's name chalked on a little blackboard on the end of a rod.

'It's a way of paging you,' Father Paul explained. 'Isn't it nicer than bellowing out some fellow's name?' He smiled his easy smile, his eyes beginning to water as a result of the few drinks he'd had. He was beginning to feel the strain: he kept thinking of their mother lying there, of what she'd say if she knew what he'd done, how she'd savagely upbraid him for keeping the fact from Francis. Out of duty and humanity he had returned each year to see her because, after all, you only had the one mother. But he had never cared for her.

Francis went for a walk after dinner. There were young soldiers with what seemed to be toy guns on the streets, but he knew the guns were real. In the shop windows there were television sets for sale, and furniture and clothes, just like anywhere else. There were advertisements for some film or other, two writhing women without a stitch on them, the kind of thing you wouldn't seen in Co. Tipperary. 'You want something, sir?' a girl said, smiling at him with broken front teeth. The siren of a police car or an ambulance shrilled urgently near by. He shook his head at the girl. 'No, I don't want anything,' he said, and then realized what she had meant. She was small and very dark, no more than a child. He hurried on, praying for her.

When he returned to the hotel he found his brother in the lounge with other people, two men and two women.

Father Paul was ordering a round of drinks, and called out to the barman to bring another whisky. 'Ah, no, no,' Francis protested, anxious to go to his room and to think about the day, to read the New Testament and perhaps to write a few more postcards. Music was playing, coming from speakers that could not be seen.

'My brother Francis,' Father Paul said to the people he was with, and the people all gave their names, adding that they came from New York. 'I was telling them about Tipp,' Father Paul said to his brother, offering his packet of cigarettes around.

'You like Jerusalem, Francis?' one of the American women asked him, and he replied that he hadn't been able to take it in yet. Then, feeling that didn't sound enthusiastic enough, he added that being there was the experience of a lifetime.

Father Paul went on talking about Co. Tipperary and then spoke of his parish in San Francisco, the boys' home and the two promising footballers, the plans for the new church. The Americans listened and in a moment the conversation drifted on to the subject of their travels in England, their visit to Istanbul and Athens, an argument they'd had with the Customs at Tel Aviv. 'Well, I think I'll hit the hay,' one of the men announced eventually, standing up.

The others stood up too and so did Francis. Father Paul remained where he was, gesturing again in the direction of the barman. 'Sit down for a nightcap,' he urged his brother.

'Ah, no, no—' Francis began.

'Bring us two more of those,' the priest ordered with a sudden abruptness, and the barman hurried away. 'Listen,' said Father Paul. 'I've something to tell you.'

After dinner, while Francis had been out on his walk, before he'd dropped into conversation with the Americans, Father Paul had said to himself that he couldn't stand the strain. It was the old woman stretched out above the hardware shop, as stiff as a board already, with the little lights burning in her room: he kept seeing all that, as if she wanted him to, as if she was trying to haunt him. Nice as the idea was, he didn't think he could continue with what he'd planned, with waiting until they got up to Galilee.

Francis didn't want to drink any more. He hadn't wanted the whisky his brother had ordered him earlier, nor the one the Americans had ordered for him. He didn't want the one that the barman now brought. He thought he'd just leave it there, hoping his brother wouldn't see it. He lifted the glass to his lips, but he managed not to drink any.

'A bad thing has happened,' Father Paul said.

'Bad? How d'you mean, Paul?'

'Are you ready for it?' he paused. Then he said, 'She died.'

Francis didn't know what he was talking about. He didn't know who was meant to be dead, or why his brother was behaving in an odd manner. He didn't like to think it but he had to: his brother wasn't fully sober.

'Our mother died,' Father Paul said. 'I'm after getting a telegram.'

The huge area that was the lounge of the Plaza Hotel, the endless tables and people sitting at them, the swiftly moving waiters and barmen, seemed suddenly a dream. Francis had a feeling that he was not where he appeared to be, that he wasn't sitting with his brother, who was wiping his lips with a handkerchief. For a moment he appeared in his confusion to be struggling his way up the Via Dolorosa again, and then in the Nativity Boutique.

'Take it easy, boy,' his brother was saying. 'Take a mouthful of whisky.'

Francis didn't obey that injunction. He asked his brother to repeat what he had said, and Father Paul repeated that their mother had died.

Francis closed his eyes and tried as well to shut away the sounds around them. He prayed for the salvation of his mother's soul. 'Blessed Virgin, intercede,' his own voice said in his mind. 'Dear Mary, let her few small sins be forgiven.'

Having rid himself of his secret, Father Paul felt instant relief. With the best of intentions, it had been a foolish idea to think he could maintain the secret until they arrived in a place that was perhaps the most suitable in the world to hear about the death of a person who'd been close to you. He took a gulp of his whisky and wiped his mouth with his handkerchief again. He watched his brother, waiting for his eyes to open.

'When did it happen?' Francis asked eventually.

'Yesterday.'

'And the telegram only came—'

'It came last night, Francis. I wanted to save you the pain.'

'Save me? How could you save me? I sent her a postcard, Paul.'

'Listen to me, Francis—'

'How could you save me the pain?'

'I wanted to tell you when we got up to Galilee.'

Again Francis felt he was caught in the middle of a dream. He couldn't understand his brother: he couldn't understand what he meant by saying a telegram had come last night, why at a moment like this he was talking about Galilee. He didn't know why he was sitting in this noisy place when he should be back in Ireland.

'I fixed the funeral for Monday,' Father Paul said.

Francis nodded, not grasping the significance of this arrangement. 'We'll be back there this time tomorrow,' he said.

'No need for that, Francis. Sunday morning's time enough.'

'But she's dead—'

'We'll be there in time for the funeral.'

'We can't stay here if she's dead.'

It was this, Father Paul realized, he'd been afraid of when he'd argued with himself and made his plan. If he had knocked on Francis's door the night before, Francis would have wanted to return immediately without seeing a single stone of the land he had come so far to be moved by.

'We could go straight up to Galilee in the morning,' Father Paul said quietly. 'You'll find comfort in Galilee, Francis.'

But Francis shook his head. 'I want to be with her,' he said.

Father Paul lit another cigarette. He nodded at a hovering waiter, indicating his need of another drink. He said to himself that he must keep his cool, an expression he was fond of.

'Take it easy, Francis,' he said.

'Is there a plane out in the morning? Can we make arrangements now?' He looked about him as if for a member of the hotel staff who might be helpful.

'No good'll be done by tearing off home, Francis. What's wrong with Sunday?'

'I want to be with her.'

Anger swelled within Father Paul. If he began to argue his words would become slurred: he knew that from experience. He must keep his cool and speak slowly and clearly, making a few simple points. It was typical of her, he though, to die inconveniently.

'You've come all this way,' he said as slowly as he could without sounding peculiar. 'Why cut it any shorter than we need? We'll be losing a week anyway. She wouldn't want us to go back.'

'I think we should.'

He was right in that. Her possessiveness in her lifetime would have reached out across a dozen continents for Francis. She'd known what she was doing by dying when she had.

'I shouldn't have come.' Francis said. 'She didn't want me to come.'

'You're thirty-seven years of age, Francis.'

'I did wrong to come.'

'You did no such thing.'

The time he'd taken her to Rome she'd been difficult for the whole week, complaining about the food, saying everywhere was dirty. Whenever he'd spent anything she'd disapproved. All his life, Father Paul felt, he'd done his best for her. He had told her before anyone else when he'd decided to enter the priesthood, certain that she'd be pleased. 'I thought you'd take over the shop,' she'd said instead.

'What difference could it make to wait, Francis?'

'There's nothing to wait for.'

As long as he lived Francis knew he would never forgive himself. As long as he lived he would say to himself that he hadn't been able to wait a few years, until she'd passed quietly on. He might even have been in the room with her when it happened.

'It was a terrible thing not to tell me,' he said. 'I sat down and wrote her a postcard, Paul. I bought her a plate.'

'So you said.'

'You're drinking too much of that whisky.'

'Now, Francis, don't be silly.'

'You're half drunk and she's lying there.'

'She can't be brought back no matter what we do.'

'She never hurt anyone,' Francis said.

Father Paul didn't deny that, although it wasn't true. She had hurt their sister Kitty, constantly reproaching her for marrying the man she had, long after Kitty was aware she'd made a mistake. She'd driven Edna to Canada after Edna, still unmarried, had had a miscarriage that only the family knew about. She had made a shadow out of Francis although Francis didn't know it. Failing to hold on to her other children, she had grasped her youngest to her, as if she had borne him to destroy him.

'It'll be you who'll say a Mass for her?' Francis said.

'Yes, of course it will.'

'You should have told me.'

Francis realized why, all day, he'd been disappointed. From the moment when the hired car had pulled into the lay-by and his brother had pointed across the valley at the Garden of Gethsemane he'd been disappointed and had not admitted it. He'd been disappointed in the Via Dolorosa and in the Church of the Holy Sepulchre and in Bethlehem. He remembered the bespectacled man who'd kept saying that you couldn't be sure about anything. All the people with cameras made it impossible to think, all the jostling and pushing was distracting. When he'd said there'd been too much to take in he'd meant something different.

'Her death got in the way,' he said.

'What d'you mean, Francis?'

'It didn't feel like Jerusalem, it didn't feel like Bethlehem.'

'But it is, Francis, it is.'

'There are soldiers with guns all over the place. And a girl came up to me on the street. There was that man with a bit of the Cross. There's you, drinking and smoking in this place—'

'Now, listen to me, Francis—'

'Nazareth would be a disappointment. And the Sea of Galilee. And the Church of the Loaves and Fishes.' His voice had risen. He lowered it again. 'I couldn't believe in the Stations this morning. I couldn't see it happening the way I do at home.'

'That's nothing to do with her death, Francis. You've got a bit of jet-lag, you'll settle yourself up in Galilee. There's an atmosphere in Galilee that nobody misses.'

'I'm not going near Galilee.' He struck the surface of the table, and Father Paul told him to contain himself. People turned their heads, aware that anger had erupted in the pale-faced man with the priest.

'Quieten up,' Father Paul commanded sharply, but Francis didn't.

'She knew I'd be better at home,' he shouted, his voice shrill and reedy. 'She knew I was making a fool of myself, a man out of a shop trying to be big—'

'Will you keep your voice down? Of course you're not making a fool of yourself.'

'Will you find out about planes tomorrow morning?'

Father Paul sat for a moment longer, not saying anything, hoping his brother would say he was sorry. Naturally it was a shock, naturally he'd be emotional and feel guilty, in a moment it would be better. But it wasn't, and Francis didn't say he was sorry. Instead he began to weep.

'Let's go up to your room,' Father Paul said, 'and I'll fix about the plane.'

Francis nodded but did not move. His sobbing ceased, and then he said, 'I'll always hate the Holy Land now.'

'No need for that, Francis.'

But Francis felt there was and he felt he would hate, as well, the brother he had admired for as long as he could remember. In the lounge of the Plaza Hotel he felt mockery surfacing everywhere. His brother's deceit, and the endless whisky in his brother's glass, and his casualness after a death seemed like the scorning of a Church which honoured so steadfastly the mother of its founder. Vivid in his mind, his own mother's eyes reminded him that they'd told him he was making a mistake, and upbraided him for not heeding her. Of course there was mockery everywhere, in the splinter of wood beneath plastic, and in the soldiers with guns that were not toys, and the writhing nakedness in the Holy City. He'd become part of it himself, sending postcards to the dead. Not speaking again to his brother, he went to his room to pray.

'Eight a.m., sir,' the girl at the reception desk said, and Father Paul asked that arrangements should be made to book two seats on the plane, explaining that it was an emergency, that a death had occurred. 'It will be all right, sir,' the girl promised.

He went slowly downstairs to the bar. He sat in a corner and lit a cigarette and ordered two whiskys and ice, as if expecting a companion. He drank them both himself and ordered more. Francis would return to Co. Tipperary and after the funeral he would take up again the life she had ordained for him. In his brown cotton coat he would serve customers with nails and hinges and wire. He would regularly go to Mass and to Confession and to Men's Confraternity. He would sit alone in the lace-curtained sitting-room, lonely for the woman who had made him what he was, married forever to her memory.

Father Paul lit a fresh cigarette from the butt of the last one. He continued to order whisky in two glasses. Already he could sense the hatred that Francis had earlier felt taking root in himself. He wondered if he would ever again return in July to Co. Tipperary, and imagined he would not.

At midnight he rose to make the journey to bed and found himself unsteady on his feet. People looked at him, thinking it disgraceful for a priest to be drunk in Jerusalem, with cigarette ash all over his clerical clothes.

The Statue

A L I C E   T H O M A S   E L L I S

*T*here has been a lot of talk recently about statues
moving. Well they *do*. I know because I once spent
Christmas in a niche. I had been shopping yet again on
the endless Christmas round and I stopped at our local
church for a sitdown more than anything else because I
was in no mood for praying. I sat there going over my
purchases in my mind and realizing I would have to go
out yet again since I had forgotten many things—wrapping paper, and cloves for the bread sauce and red apples
for the centre of the table and more mundane things like
cats' meat and toothpaste. As I collected my carrier bags
and genuflected preparatory to leaving I glanced to my
left and caught the gaze of our local saint; her melli-
fluous, impartial and, as I now thought, annoyingly
smug gaze.

'It's all right for you,' I told her. 'Stuck up there out of
the way in your plastered peace with your self-satisfied
smirk.' I would never have spoken like that normally but
my feet were hurting and my arms were nearly dragged
out of their sockets with the weight of the shopping. It

was freezing outside too. Still, there was no excuse for being rude to a saint so I apologized in an undertone, and then just as I turned to go I saw her eyes look swiftly to the left and right and then she put her painted plaster finger to her painted plaster mouth and leaned forwards towards me. Naturally I was astounded. I dropped one of my bags and heard something break and I gripped the back of a pew for support. Luckily there were very few other people in the church, only one or two old women rapt in contemplation of Our Lady and a comatose wino laid out on the floor. All the same, at my reaction she straightened up and resumed her stance in her niche, gazing into the distance with her small smile. After a moment I addressed her again. 'Did you just move,' I demanded, in a whisper, 'or am I going mad on top of everything else?' Her eyes flickered down at me and her smile widened. I sat on the pew and looked sideways and up at her, and then I heard her speak. The gist of what she said was this: that she would carry my shopping home and take my place over Christmas if I would agree to take her place in the niche. Well, it wasn't exactly up to my dream of spending Christmas alone in a small snowbound hotel at the end of the world, but it would certainly mean a rest, so I hardly hesitated at all before agreeing and the next thing I knew I was looking across the church from the saint's erstwhile vantage point with my eyes on a level with the seventh Station of the Cross and a weary-looking woman was gathering up a lot of carrier bags and genuflecting below my feet. As she left she smiled up at me reassuringly and told me not to worry, she would take very good care of everyone and everything of mine. I had a moment's misgiving because my motives in agreeing to this imposture had been completely selfish, arising from my great tiredness, from the prospect of for once being spared Uncle Fred's Christmas jokes, Cousin Amy's dissatisfaction with the arrangements no matter what they might be, and the early morning riot as the children tore the wrappings from their presents and discovered that I had forgotten to buy batteries to motivate their robots, toy cars, radios, etc. But then I reflected that my family could hardly be in better hands than those of a canonized saint and that if I had any sense I would stop worrying and make the most of my rest. It would be ungrateful to spend Christmas fretting about those things I had left undone. I hoped the saint would be inspired to check the store cupboards and discover the lack of cloves. Bread sauce without cloves is insipid. Then I began to relax. The cat would point out unhesitatingly the lack of cats' meat; if anyone could not get by without toothpaste then they could hasten out and buy some. I felt the saint could be trusted to choose some decorative motif for the table centre, and as for the wrapping paper—well, I found I really didn't care about that any more. I was perfectly comfortable standing in the niche because, after all, I had no bone or muscle to strain or stretch, being composed of plaster and paint on a wire armature, and I felt warm and secure in the silence which was stirred only by an occasional shuffle of ancient feet, a cough, a murmured incantation. I clutched my handful of plaster hyacinths (the saint's most potent emblem) and gazed with her own tranquillity across the aisles, my foot resting gently on a plaster boar's head.

Suddenly I became aware that someone was addressing me. I cautiously lowered my gaze and saw the top of a woman's head, nodding slowly up and down. '... I wouldn't want him to suffer,' she was saying, 'not

too much anyway, for when he hasn't the drink taken
he's been good enough to me.' At this she looked up,
her eyes met mine and I recognized her as my next-door
neighbour's cleaning lady. Simultaneously I realized
that she was invoking the help of her whom she
believed to be the saint, to procure the death of her
husband; had probably been doing a novena to this end,
and I felt very much taken aback although not entirely
surprised. The saint, you see, had gained her eminence
in the community of saints not merely by the exemplary
virtue of her ways but because she had been married by
force to a perfect brute who used to beat her and tie her
to trees and fling her down into dungeons because she
utterly refused to fulfil her conjugal obligations. One
day while he was chasing her round the woods she ran
into a wild boar who gored her to death; only just before
she expired in a handy bed of hyacinths she forgave her
husband his importunities, cruelties and misdemean-
ours, and he repented and mended his ways amazingly,
becoming a highly respected member of society and
exceedingly devout. I was aware that some uneducated
women, misunderstanding this tale and forgetting the
saint's magnanimity and remembering only the horrible ways of her husband, were in the habit of asking
her for assistance in marital matters, but I had not
realized that anyone could be so misguided as to seek
her intercession to the extent of asking for the death of
a spouse. My shock must have shown on my face for I
felt my jaw drop and at that moment the woman looked
imploringly up at me. My fingers momentarily relaxed
and I felt a hyacinth slip from between them. Of course,
the woman shrieked. I knew just how she felt. If I
hadn't been so tired I might have shrieked myself when

the saint spoke to me. The woman fled up the aisle to the door and a moment later she was back, dragging the curate with her. He had clearly been interrupted in the course of his tea for he was eating bread and jam, and had the reluctant air of a curate who knows that the cake will have been eaten by the time he returns.

'Look,' said the woman dramatically, pointing at the wretched hyacinth.

'It's only a hyacinth,' said the curate. The clergy are notoriously sceptical about miraculous happenings. They have to be.

'*She* dropped it on me,' insisted the woman, pointing up at me while I strove very hard to keep in countenance, much regretting my lapse although I felt I could not be held wholly to blame since she had greatly startled me. One does not expect one's neighbour's char to nurture murderous inclinations towards her husband, or at least not to be so open and frank about them. I had to remind myself that she supposed me to be the saint and not her employer's neighbour but I still considered the behaviour indiscreet.

She and the curate argued this way and that and the tone of their discussion became quite heated. I stood in some embarrassment, vowing to be more careful until Christmas had passed. When I was alone again, reflecting on the nature of marriage, I had another worrying thought. My husband was an uxorious man and in view of the saint's attitude to conjugality I could see the possibility of serious misunderstanding. I hoped she would have the foresight to develop a heavy cold and insist on sleeping in the spare room.

The next morning as the congregation arrived for Mass I kept a wary eye on the door to see the saint enter in the guise of myself. She had brought the two older children and I was relieved to see that her—my—nose was scarlet and our eyes were streaming. After Mass she came over to speak to me. In between a muttered Ave and a Paternoster and over the clicking of the beads she whispered reassurances to me about the state of the house and the children's appetites and my husband's health. Even the cat, it seemed, had accepted her without question. I longed to ask her if she had remembered to buy the cloves but after the events of the afternoon I dared not and stood smiling vacantly as she spoke to me in my own voice.

'Come *on*, Mummy,' said my children, pulling at my skirt which the saint wore and I felt a tremor in my plaster toes until I reminded myself that Mummy was, for the moment, not I but the tired-looking woman below with the dreadful cold.

'Goodbye, hyacinth lady,' said the younger of the two older children and I was glad to see that I—she— punished this affection with a little shake. Relieved of anxiety about my family I reverted to worrying about my neighbour's char. She was a nice, hard-working woman with many children and, as had now become evident, a husband so unbearable that she wished him dead. I would not have been so concerned had she not confided in me, for although she did not know that I had her secret I felt strangely responsible for her. She came to look at me again on her way home from work, standing at my feet and gazing up at me with an expression of half-fearful expectancy. I was dreadfully tempted to speak to her, to offer her—not comfort, for I could think of none—but advice. I wanted to tell her to go to a marriage guidance counsellor although I knew that the fact that she had come to me—or rather the saint—meant that if this idea had occurred to her she had rejected it. She looked at me imploringly for a little while longer and then left, her poor shoulders bowed with worry and disappointment and the prospect of a beating from her husband and I seethed in my niche with indignation and pity.

The next day was Christmas Eve and the saint called to see me in the afternoon with two of the younger children. She sat in the pew below me while the children went to look at the crib—at the lambs and the donkey and the star. She whispered that everything was ready for tomorrow, the capon stuffed, the potatoes peeled, the oyster soup ready to be reheated. Yes, she said kindly, she knew she must be sure and let it boil, she promised she wouldn't let my family suffer from food poisoning—not even Uncle Fred or Cousin Amy. I was glad to see she had a sense of humour and relieved that she seemed to have a good grasp of the basic rules of cookery. This worry had not occurred to me before but as she had flourished some centuries ago I would not have been surprised had she confessed an inability to master the intricacies of the gas stove, the food processor, washing-machine, etc. I wondered if she'd been driving the car. The evening passed peacefully and I stood, half-dreaming, content in my niche while one or two people asked my intercession in more reasonable matters—a girl wished to visit the Costa Brava and an old man wanted to win some money on a horse. I made a note to pass these requests on to the saint when we resumed our normal roles and personae. As the time for Midnight Mass approached I watched the saint come in with all my family, even Uncle Fred and Cousin Amy, right down to the baby who peered at me over his father's shoulder with every sign of approval. Taking a chance, I blew him a swift kiss and he remarked 'poggelich bah' and laughed.

'Sh,' said my husband.

'Pooh,' said my child, beaming at me. I pulled myself together and stood quite still, gazing over their heads at the far wall.

Halfway through Mass there was a slight disturbance at the back of the church as some latecomers arrived. From the stumbling and slurred mutterings I gathered that they were drunk. This happened every year. Certain men who never attended Mass at any other time, not even to make their Easter Duties, would invariably, inevitably, roll up, paralytic, for Midnight Mass. Nobody minded as long as they weren't sick and didn't swear too loudly as they fell over attempting to kneel unsupported on the floor. One of them reeled unsteadily down the aisle and came to a halt below my niche. He clutched the end of the pew and knelt down. As he did so I caught sight of his face and recognized him despite the crossed eyes and hectically flushed nose as the husband of my neighbour's char. I glared down at him before recalling myself to the Mass. When it was over and the sleepy congregation made its slow way to the doors I saw that he had fallen fast asleep leaning against the pew's end. No one made any move to disturb him, but left unanimously by way of the centre aisle as he slumped there, snoring gently, and suddenly I was seized by an irresistible compulsion. Cautiously I loosened yet another hyacinth and dropped it on his head. He woke disoriented, half-blind with beer and sleep, and looked round pugnaciously. Whereupon I leaned swiftly forward, seized him by the collar so that he was forced to look into my face, and remarked in a low but positive tone, 'If you don't stop drinking and beating your wife, you bastard, you will be very, very sorry.' Then I dropped him and stood back in the niche, stone-still and silent. I heard later that he had left the church, gone home and kissed his wife and all his children, thrown away the cans of beer he was keeping in the sideboard, helped wash up after Christmas dinner and taken his whole family for an outing on Boxing Day. His wife never knew exactly what had happened but she was delighted. When he stopped drinking he was able to go back to being a builder's labourer and he made so much money that she was able to give up her job cleaning for my neighbour and stay at home washing his labouring clothes. My neighbour was very put out but I felt that that really couldn't be helped.

The saint came back the day after Boxing Day. I thought that she—I—looked very tired but she seemed content and said that she had left everything as she imagined I would wish to find it and Cousin Amy had not been too obnoxious. There were quite a few leftovers still, but she was sure I would be able to sort everything out when I got home. She apologized that the bread sauce had been a bit tasteless because she hadn't been able to find my cloves but everything else had been very good. When she was back in her niche and I in my self I thought that she looked rather relieved, and I was a bit annoyed to find that she had left me with the remains of her cold, although she had got over the initial worst stages of sore throat, raw chest and itching nose.

I found the house remarkably tidy, with an unusual air of order and propriety; the children cheerful and amiable. Only the baby was sitting in his pram, thumb in mouth, looking puzzled and faintly forlorn. When I picked him up he looked at me for a long moment, then took his thumb out of his mouth, put his arms around my neck and would not be parted from me until he fell asleep long past his bedtime when the moon was high.

Friends, Strangers, Brothers

F R A N C E S   F U L L E R

*B*ecause Abdu lived by principle and refused to be stopped at the occupation army's checkpoint, Malcolm drove around the hill and down to the orchard alone, hauling the boxes they would need.

It was soon after dawn when they threw the wooden crates into the trunk and back seat of Malcolm's car, and Abdu set his clay water jug in the front seat and started walking down the slope. The morning was radiant with goodness, the sun spilling over the opposite mountain but not yet reaching the wadi, the forests still full of blue shadows. A flock of black goats clattered across the road, raised a cloud of dust, and started nibbling among the weeds and thorns. For a few moments Malcolm sat behind the wheel of his car, smelling the dust, the bitter weeds and occasional whiffs of manure, enjoying the expectation of simple work and the idea that he and Abdu could be a team, harvesting the plums. He watched his friend, tall and gaunt and deliberate, descending along a zig-zag path, stepping carefully through a vegetable patch and skirting a vineyard before he dropped over the terrace wall and disappeared among the pine trees.

Malcolm spent most of his life behind a desk or a lectern, but he was drawn to men who tilled the ground and was secretly envious of those who worked in the sun and wore callouses on their hands. *By the intelligence of such men, we all live*, he thought, staring at the spot where Abdu had entered the woods, and behind the thought, a mere suggestion of fear slinked through his mind, the fear that economic professors did not contribute anything essential to the world.

There was nothing frightening or difficult about passing the roadblock so far as Malcolm could see. The soldier looked at him closely, then motioned him to proceed. Abdu's obstinacy seemed like useless pride, but because it was Abdu, Malcolm assumed he must have a good reason. For a year or more he had not been to his own land by road, choosing instead to carry loads of fruits and vegetables up the mountainside on his shoulders.

The little road, which had been black-topped years ago but was now full of chuckholes, wound through a snobar forest and down into the morning shadows of mountain bluffs, toward the little dirt trail that led to Abdu's plum trees. The pines, the fruit trees, everything looked small, because of the way the canyon walls hovered on both sides. Malcolm felt small.

By the time he reached the orchard, Abdu was there, walking around, inspecting his fruit, not looking small at all, but like a giant scarecrow with oversized hands, loose trousers, and a leather face slashed with crevices.

Immediately the two men put the boxes on the ground under the first row of trees and began to reach into the branches to grasp the purple fruit and then to stoop and roll it off their fingers, gently, into the boxes.

They worked silently; none of their usual discussions of politics. If they were sitting at Malcolm's kitchen table or on Abdu's back patio, Malcolm would ask Abdu his opinion about the president's latest trip to neighbouring capitals, even though Abdu's interpretations often seemed far-fetched to him. Actually, he didn't even like to talk politics, and he was aware that, just as Abdu's thoughts were illogical to him, his own were naive to Abdu. Yet they talked politics; it was a contagious compulsion, epidemic in Lebanon.

Right away the day grew hot. Bees and flies hummed, searching for broken fruit and oozing juice. Under the plum trees the air was still and heavy with odours—fruit, dust, vinegar, decay. Malcolm stood on a box more frequently than Abdu, because he was shorter. And Abdu, who never hurried and never wasted any effort, had filled his first box when Malcolm's was half full.

'Slow down,' the American said. 'You're making me look lazy.'

'Never mind, Ustaz. I'm used to this.' Abdu always called him 'professor,' out of genuine respect for his education, while Malcolm could never find an adequate way to express his esteem for Abdu, a man his own age who always seemed both younger and older, more expert in the art of living.

They stopped for a drink from Abdu's jug, Malcolm already turning pink from the sun, and agreed that they were hot and there was a foulness in the air. For a while they went on working, but as the temperature rose, the impression of something rotten came on relentlessly, breath after breath, like a sinister shadow approaching through the trees.

'There is something dead here,' Abdu decided, his nostrils quivering. And as he finished the branch he was stripping with his big hands, he began to glance over his shoulders and between the rows.

'Maybe a dog?' Malcolm said, and finally Abdu ambled, stooping under the limbs, to the end of the row. Malcolm saw him lean to peer at something on the ground, then motion for him to come.

As Malcolm approached, Abdu spoke softly, 'It's not a dog. Come see.'

Malcolm followed him to where the soldier lay among the clods and stones and summer weeds. His mouth was open, as if he had called for help or cried out in pain. Death had made the gesture gross by preserving it. A fly buzzed in and out of the blue cavity. Though his body was expressionless now, like a stone or a jar, a thing, an empty thing, he could not have been dead many hours. Youthfulness had not yet departed from his face. His uniform bore the insignia of the occupation army.

Abdu and Malcolm stood over the body and looked at one another. They began to speak in whispers, their voices smaller than the insects'.

'How did he get here?' Malcolm asked.

'I don't know.'

'Who could have killed him?'

'They kill them,' Abdu said. 'The militias. Every night one or two.'

'Was he shot?'

'I don't see the wound.' He leaned, pinched the soldier's sleeve in his fingers and lifted the body until they saw black blood on the back of his shirt. 'Here it is. Knifed in the back, but I think it happened somewhere else. There's not enough blood here.'

'Look in his pockets. Does he have an i.d.?'

Abdu dropped the dead man's sleeve, and the body rolled back like a log. 'We don't want to know who he is.'

'Why? What must we do?'

'We have to hide him, get rid of him.'

'But shouldn't we report it to someone?'

The sudden lifting of Abdu's eyebrows would have been answer enough, but he added, 'My sons are in the militia, and this body is on my land.'

'Bashir and Hanni would be...?' He wanted to say 'implicated,' but his Arabic failed him, so he said, 'Would be in trouble?'

'Of course. Big trouble.' He turned his back and with a gesture called Malcolm to follow him to the place where they had been working. He started picking plums again. 'I have to think,' he said, 'but keep picking plums.'

His long, leathery face was expressionless and calm, and Malcolm remembered the day when they were sitting on Abdu's patio, drinking mulberry juice, and heard a shell come whistling across the canyon in front of them and crash nearby. Malcolm had tensed to leap from his chair, but Abdu had not even blinked. He pointed to a billow of dust on the far hill. 'The gun is over there,' he said. And jerking his thumb toward a burst of smoke on their left, 'The shell hit there.'

Abdu rolled a handful of plums into the dark heap in the box at his feet, stood up and said in a loud whisper, 'Listen. These soldiers get ambushed at their posts. Sometimes they just disappear. I don't know who does it. I know, but not specifically who. You understand?'

'The militias are trying to drive them away, I know. But what are we going to do?'

'I'll go for kerosene. We'll burn it.'

'But if you and Bashir or Hanni went to the army and reported the body, wouldn't that prove they were not guilty?'

'It would prove nothing,' Abdu hissed. 'They are guilty whether they did it or not.'

'Wouldn't it be better just to bury him, then?'

'This ground is too hard and rocky. We couldn't put him deep enough. And we don't have that much time.'

Malcolm knew finally that Abdu was afraid and became afraid himself. Soldiers were camped around the curve of the hill, a kilometre away, the same soldiers he had driven past two hours ago and must drive past again today. Even now they might be looking for this man.

'Stay,' Abdu said. 'Stay here, pick plums. No. Find sticks, dead branches, anything. Cover the body. Then pick plums. No one must know, Ustaż. No one.'

Malcolm expected him to leave running, but he began to walk in his usual calm dignity, except he hesitated once, came back and hoisted a box of plums onto his shoulder.

Malcolm began darting this way and that, grabbing anything burnable in sight. Abdu was right; it was the only way. They owed nothing to the enemy, not even to such a young enemy. But he was already feeling dirty and deceitful, because of Emily. He could not tell her about this. She had reflex feelings about lost soldiers, understandably. She would get upset, and no matter how he explained it, he would go down another notch in her eyes.

This is how it happens, he thought, *that honest people develop lists of things they can't talk about and start hiding things about themselves*. As he thought this, he was searching for broken limbs and tearing at the brown thornbushes, trying to pull them up with his bare hands. There was so little brush, and before he had half covered the body, he heard voices and rushed back to the other end of the row and began picking plums again. Two men were coming, one of them calling Abdu.

'Welcome,' he greeted them, trying to be casual and cheerful. 'Abdu is not here; he went up to his house.' His voice trembled. He was sure it would betray him. The smell was obvious now. Could one talk enough to keep people from noticing a smell?

One of the men was a local taxi driver, whom Malcolm recognized. He stood with his hands in his pockets, jingling his car keys. 'My passenger needs to see Abdu.'

The other was a short man, shorter even than Malcolm, who tilted his chin up and looked at the world through half-closed eyelids. This habit made him appear to be suspicious. The two men stood there, watching him pick plums, listening to him talking, too much and too fast, saying that they had just missed him, and he would probably be gone for quite a while, and Malcolm became self-conscious about his movements. He was not experienced in harvesting fruit; maybe this was evident to them. Then the short man with the suspicious eyes said, 'Something smells bad here.'

Malcolm thought, *I knew it. A Lebanese will never miss a smell, especially if it's bad.*

He said, 'Yes, there is a dead dog.'

Then the taxi driver took a couple of steps toward the inside of the orchard and said, 'Or maybe...'

'Never mind. We found it. Abdu went to bring kerosene so we can burn it.'

The driver turned around, took his hands out of his pockets and said to his client, 'We'll catch him up the hill.' It sounded like he was saying that they were obviously unwanted.

Malcolm could feel his heart pounding in his throat; He was not sure he had said the right thing. He kept picking plums, in case they should look back.

Once he had brought home a bone from the rubble of Tel asZatar, a thigh bone. It was long after the battle there; sunshine streamed in through devastated walls, and silence filled the little tunnels where people had hidden during the siege. Emily had been horrified that he would handle it, would bring it into their house. She acted personally offended. Without saying so, she made him feel that he was not the man she had thought.

'It's only a bone,' he had said.

'It is part of a human being,' she had replied.

Thinking that a shadow had passed overhead, Malcolm looked up and saw two big birds circling. Vultures had found the carcass. Wouldn't vultures be a signal to anyone looking for the body? He wished Abdu would come.

He left the box of plums and took another armful of dry twigs over to the body and stood there holding them, looking down into a face now stiff and ugly. The horror of finding this corpse came down on him like an illness. Now the innocent were afraid. And now they really were responsible for something. What they did and didn't do would alter life forever for someone. It was not right, he was sure it was not right to burn him without knowing his name, without making it possible for his family to know that he was dead. He threw down the trash and, with a glance over his shoulder, squatted and began searching the soldier's pockets. The smell was getting stronger in the heat, and he wished he could hold his breath. He found a few coins in a front pocket and rolled the body part way to reach the hip pocket, where he found a small wallet. Inside were a few tattered papers and a plasticized card. Quickly he stuffed these into his own hip pocket and put the wallet under the body.

On the terrace below, he found a rotten log, and managed to drag it up and tilt it across the dead boy's chest.

After an age, Abdu arrived with a cardboard box on his shoulder. In the box he had kindling wood, kerosene and matches, even a small hatchet. 'I heard,' he said, 'that we found a dead dog.' He seemed pleased.

Malcolm looked away quickly, realizing suddenly that he had insulted a man by calling him a dog. He intended to give him dignity again by rescuing his name from destruction, but his friend must now know.

He said, 'Look,' pointing at the vultures.

'I saw them. They will go away soon.'

While Malcolm watched, Abdu doused everything with kerosene, the clothes, the skin, the hair, such hair as there was. Those kids were all practically skinned. Then he went to work, slicing the log expertly with the hatchet, placing each piece of wood, according to design, using the twigs and brush that Malcolm had piled up.

'When I make charcoal,' he said, 'I build a pyramid of wood, and it burns for two days. We want this to burn quickly and very hot.' His hands might have been shaking slightly.

Malcolm said, 'Too bad, you know; he was just a boy.'

'It's too late for pity.'

'Sure.' He tried to keep his voice casual. 'I was just

thinking that he must have a family. I was wondering what you would want someone else to do, if Bashir or Hanni were lying dead in enemy territory.'

Abdu got still for a moment, squatting on his heel, and then went back to work without looking at him. 'I can tell you what would happen if Bashir or Hanni were lying dead in our brother's field.'

It was a habit people had formed, to call the occupiers 'brothers'. The word implied bitterly the lack of choices left to the Lebanese ('We choose our friends.'), covered enmity with levity and could be spoken anywhere without fear.

'They would take the watch from his arm, the money from his pocket, the shoes from his feet, the gold from his teeth, and then they would throw him to the coyotes. He would be eaten by the beasts. And no one would tell me he was dead.'

'You would never know?'

'I could guess.'

'My wife's brother was lost in Vietnam. He was never reported dead, but he never came home.'

'That's the way war is.'

'But it's very cruel. It killed his father slowly. My wife has never recovered, not really.'

Abdu poured kerosene on the wood he had piled over the body. Then he carried the can nearly to the other end of the small orchard and set it down. Coming back, he took a little box of matches from his pocket, struck one and tossed it into the pile, which exploded into flames. Until the instant he did it, Malcolm hoped he wouldn't. The two of them jumped backwards and stood staring at the fire, feeling the heat on their faces, the harsh kerosene smoke in their lungs.

Without taking his gaze from the fire, Abdu said, 'Ustaz, I want to ask you. How can a man do what's right and the world the way it is?'

Flames were searing the limbs of two plum trees. The leaves were curling, the fruit peel frying and bursting. The smell of death was already replaced by other smells—fire, scorched fruit, burned cloth.

Malcolm said, 'Maybe we should have moved him farther away.'

Abdu said, 'Ma'leish. Never mind,' with profound resignation.

Malcolm was aware he had not answered a question, but he did not know what to say. He felt a subtle pressure in the area of his hip pocket, wondering what it was, exactly, that he had hidden there, and how he would use it. Maybe it would offer a way to cleanse himself.

They stood there, friends and strangers, caught together in a trap, while he plotted to escape alone. The thought made him feel soiled and worried. He did not want to betray this good man, his favourite neighbour.

He said, 'How long does it take a body to burn?'

'I don't know. I have never done this before.'

'Do they send patrols down this road?'

'Never. They're scared.'

They went back to picking plums, which were purple and smooth and firm. Occasionally they ate one. They filled most of the boxes they had brought with them. The orchard was full of wood smoke, an odour of kerosene and the stink of burning hair and flesh. The first black smoke dissipated, and a gray haze floated up the hillside, obscuring a vineyard, rising through the pine trees towards the fields and houses of the village. Everyone would know they had built a fire.

'Be careful what you say about this,' Abdu told him. 'They have agents everywhere.'

'Even in the village?'

'Even in the village. Some of them we know. But there must be others. And careless people who talk.'

Malcolm kept picking plums, slowly, but Abdu seemed to read his thoughts, He said, 'Remember, Ustaz, what kind of people we are dealing with. You know that boy from the Abu Joudeh family? He's in prison because they didn't like his haircut.'

'Yes. He was driving with a girl. The soldier at a checkpoint said, "That's a very short haircut," and the kid, he was just a dumb eighteen-year-old, said, "It's a marine cut." And the soldiers took him, car and all. They put the girl out on the road. For six months no one knew where the boy was. Finally, the parents paid an officer a big bribe for the information that he's in a certain prison in Damascus. A haircut, Ustaz! If a marine haircut means you're a marine, what about a body on my land?'

They heaved boxes of fruit into the car. When the fire began to smoulder they added more fuel, and there was a new billow of black smoke. The sun was straight overhead, and Malcolm was soaked with sweat and exhausted. He drank too much water and accused Abdu of being part camel, because he was not thirsty.

When they sat down to rest, Abdu seemed satisfied. Hugging his big, bony knees, he said, 'Without doubt, he was a Muslim. That shouldn't make it any better, I know, but it does, because I can't imagine them. Christians in any country are my brothers. Real brothers. They go to church and pray for their sons. Muslims, I don't know. They care, I'm sure, but I can't feel with them.'

Malcolm was surprised by this frankness and, though he liked it and though he wanted to protest, he did not think of anything solid on which to hang an argument. Instead he asked, 'What will their army do, if they keep losing men like this?'

'Probably they'll hit us really good.'

They sat for a while, imagining that.

Finally Abdu said, 'Your wife will be expecting you for lunch. Right?'

'Yes. She probably expected me before now.'

'Yalla. Go then.'

'I don't like leaving you before this is finished.'

'Ma'leish, it might take a long time. Leave the boxes in the car until I come. I'll help you unload them. Except the one in the seat, near the left door. I chose those for Emily.'

'It's more than we can eat.'

'They will keep a long time. Just don't tell your wife how hard I made you work for them.'

Malcolm looked up at Abdu to be sure he had understood the message. 'Don't worry. Emily will never know.'

Abdu walked to the car with him. 'Be careful at the roadblock.'

'They never bother me. I'm just a dumb foreigner.'

Their eyes met and held, and Malcolm saw both weariness and its acceptance in the eyes of his friend. He started to turn away, but Abdu held out a hand to stop him and said, 'You are a good man, Ustaz, and I love you very much. My sons love you. They always tell me that.'

'Thank you. You are our best friends in the village.'

'I'm depending on you, Ustaz, to keep our secret.' His hand gripping Malcolm's was dry and calloused and powerful.

'Of course,' he said, already opening the car door and feeling like a traitor. Why had he taken the soldier's papers except that he meant to tell someone?

When he got into the car, his feet felt slow, the steering wheel rigid. He wished he could stop somewhere and think before going home. The decision he had to make seemed to get more complicated by the moment, and, preoccupied with it, he forgot to think at all about the checkpoint. He was almost there when he remembered the papers in his hip pocket. It was too late to hide them. And suddenly he noticed that his hands were scratched and bloody from pulling on the thorns, though why it should matter, he didn't know.

The soldier took a long look at him, the same as the other one had when he came in the morning. Malcolm tried to look back at him calmly, tried to notice things like the man's careless uniform, his blue eyes and sunburned face, his rifle hanging casually over his shoulder. Beside him in the road another soldier stood with his rifle ready. He had a groggy look and had not shaved for two or three days. The two of them stared at him, one moving his hand on the rifle, deliberately. There was no traffic. Only Malcolm.

'Where you come from?' the blue-eyed soldier said, in English.

'From my friend's orchard.'

'Where you go?'

'To my house in the village.'

'Passport,' holding out his hand.

Malcolm leaned and took his passport from the pocket in the dash. The soldier stared at the information in the front. He looked at Malcolm and back at his picture. Then he turned a page and stared at his visas, his entrance and exit stamps. The woods were very quiet. Three hundred yards away, on the main road, a truck backfired. The soldier with the rifle ready flinched and fidgeted. The car was like an oven.

'What you do here?'

'I'm a teacher.'

'Out,' he said, tossing his head to demonstrate, and the other supported the command with a motion of his rifle. Malcolm got out, feeling sweat trickling from his armpits.

The soldier took him to the rear of the car and made a motion like lifting the trunk lid, and Malcolm knew that he had to go back for the key. His knees were shaking. He had to turn his back on the soldier, and then was horrified to realize that he had put his hand to his hip pocket and pushed down on the contents.

They lifted the trunk lid and looked at the boxes of plums and into the small space behind them. The second soldier, meanwhile, got into the front seat and rummaged through the pocket, then got out, opened the rear door and stuck his head in. When he emerged, he had four or five plums in his hand.

'Ruuh,' they told him. 'Go.'

Malcolm fumbled the keys into the ignition and managed to leave. His heart felt like an animal throwing itself against the bars of a cage, and his face was burning from the heat of his fear. *Thank God*, he thought. He wished he could laugh, but it was too soon. He thought he would enjoy telling Abdu that they were stupid men at the checkpoint, but he could not tell Abdu why he was afraid. And on second thoughts, he was the first one who had been stupid.

Getting ready to shower before lunch, he locked the bathroom door. He never did that. His clothes smelled like fire. His hands trembled when he pulled the papers out of his pocket and put them on the counter beside the sink. A soldier's 'personal effects', things that were sent to families when men died far from home. Though he could read Arabic a little, the scribbling on the scraps of paper was difficult. One paper was a form of some kind. With patience he would be able to figure it out. The plasticized card was an identification document. It had the soldier's name, his mother's name, his religion, the place and date of his birth.

As soon as he read it he knew that Abdu had been right. It was a mistake to know these things. There was no way to find a family in a big city with so little information, no way anyone could try without bringing suspicion on himself. And now there was no way to forget this name.

He tore the papers into tiny pieces and dropped them into the waste basket, under some of Emily's tissues.

The card was thick and stiff, and he did not know yet what to do with it. Obviously he couldn't carry it around, and he couldn't let Emily find it. Maybe he could hide it in one of his books. She never read his economics books. But she did pick them up and clean the edges.

After his bath, when he started to put on his slippers, he noticed that the inside lining of the left one was loose, and on an impulse he slipped the card under the lining. Then he took the slipper to his desk and glued the lining back in place. The slippers were very old. One day when he was burning trash, he would throw them in.

He went downstairs and kissed Emily without looking at her. She said, 'Did you have a good time?'

'We worked hard,' he said, hoping she was not listening closely.

141

'What was burning down there?'

This casual questioning felt like having his pockets searched, but he managed to tell himself that it wasn't her fault. 'We made a fire. We found a dead dog and burned him with a bunch of brush and junk.' *Something a lot worse than bringing home a thigh bone*, he added to himself.

'Good grief! You poisoned the whole village to get rid of a dead dog.' She said it with good humour, while pouring steaming vegetables into a bowl.

He was pondering Abdu's question which he had never answered. Can a man do what's right?

She said, 'The plums are beautiful, but as usual Abdu gave us too many.'

'Make jam. Share them with someone.' He heard the tonelessness, the indifference in his own voice. He was thinking that maybe someday, given time to put it all together, he could help her understand about her brother. But probably not.

All the while, she was saying something about their not being the right plums for jam and telling him he looked exhausted.

He sat at the table, facing the window. Smoke still covered the lower part of the hill, and the whole world smelled like burned flesh. Or maybe it smelled that way only to those who knew. Abdu must be sitting there, staring at the fire, waiting for the bones to become ashes, thinking that he had fallen into the hands of his foolish American friend and must trust him, because he had no alternative. Malcolm felt then that a lock snapped shut inside of him, and he visualized a chain, running down the hill, dropping over terrace walls, lying in the dark soil of vegetable patches, sliding around tree trunks, linking himself to the man who sat by the fire. He would never escape this chain; it could stretch to the ends of the earth without breaking. Nor would he have peace. But he would be a friend. He would protect Abdu's sons. And he would never burden this good man with the truth that it was a Christian boy from Aleppo whom they burned in the orchard.

He remembered a silly thing that kids in his high school used to say when they had offended someone. 'Excuse me for living,' they said. Like a lot of silly things, it was almost right. Being alive, one had to ask forgiveness.

A Fool For Love, After All

P A U L I N E   F I S K

I came home and peeled myself out of my black clothes, wishing I hadn't worn them because they reminded me of too many things about the princess which I'd rather not remember. My room was full of Christmas greeting cards which I should have posted yesterday, and half-hung tinsel. I looked at the black clothes thrown across the bed. Downstairs, the mince-pies awaited me, but how could I get on with them when all these memories had started flooding back?

I cleared a chair and sat down. It was snowing outside, white flakes sliding down the window-pane. She hadn't been a real princess, of course. Her name was Anna Chertkova, and she was a Russian, and she had lived next door. We children had called her that because she was a mystery.

I reached to switch on the electric fire, and the parcel which the solicitor had given me slipped off my lap. I picked it up. An envelope was tucked in its string, and I slid it out. The parcel was frayed at the edges, but the envelope had been written recently. It was addressed to me.

I opened it reluctantly. The letter inside, too, was addressed to me. I unfolded it.

'It ends as it began,' it said. 'Perhaps I've always been behind bars. And what for this time? For love, I suppose. A fool for love, after all...'

I closed my eyes, and remembered.

I was twelve years old and standing in Miss Chertkova's hall in my dressing gown and nightdress, torn between terror and almighty curiosity because down our street Miss Chertkova was God and the Queen rolled into one.

'Come into the kitchen,' she called in that foreign voice of hers which had this way of going up and down, like a song. 'Don't just stand there. You'll catch a cold. What do you drink before you go to bed?'

I scuttled down the hall, entering a kitchen with a concrete floor and the sort of stone sink that my dad had removed from our identical but so-different house next door. There were no pictures anywhere, no pretty things. A mop and pail in a corner. A smell of household soap.

'I drink cocoa,' I whispered, shrinking against the wall.

Miss Chertkova lit a prehistoric gas stove. Her face was stone-white, and her eyes were stone-cold, and she was dressed in black. I couldn't help but shiver. What was she thinking of as she looked at me? I slid a box of biscuits onto the table, but couldn't bring myself to explain that they were a present from my mum for letting me stay while our house was full of visitors.

Miss Chertkova opened the biscuits and offered me one. She stooped over the stove and made the cocoa, pouring it into a china cup and handing it to me, saying she'd show me where I was sleeping. I followed her upstairs. The wallpaper looked as if it hadn't been changed for years. The skirting boards and picture rails were dusty. The house smelt dry and crisp and cold. It was like a set piece on a stage—you couldn't believe anyone lived in it. My bedroom contained an iron bed, made up with white cotton sheets and layers of blankets. There were no curtains at the windows, no carpets on the floor.

I put my cocoa on the bedside table. Next to it, a small vase of flaming marigolds provided the only colour in the whole room.

'The marigold that goes to bed with the sun, and with him rises weeping,' Miss Chertkova said. Her voice was sad, her stooping frame stood before the flowers, shadowing them. '*The Winter's Tale*. You may have done it in school.' She switched on the bedside light, turned down the sheets. 'I hope you sleep all right,' she said. 'If you want anything, I'm along the landing.'

And she was gone.

I laid out my Sunday-best clothes for the morning, and got into bed, wishing I was back home. The mattress was lumpy and sagged so low that I wondered how I was ever going to get out again. I threw most of the blankets off the bed and fell into a tossing and turning state of half sleep, only to awaken early.

It was before six, and already light. My body ached from top to toe. I hauled myself out of bed hoping my parents never had visitors again—at least not so many of them—and a sound caught my attention; something mournful and low outside the window and I couldn't make out what it was.

I crossed the room and leaned out over the window-sill. It was a lovely morning, soft and still, all the colours of the garden blurred and mellow because the sun hadn't quite risen to make them shine. I looked down. Someone moved along the covered walk-way underneath me. I could see feet, and hear a voice.

Suddenly, Miss Chertkova emerged into view, buried in a huge old coat and swaying as she walked, lost in recitation.

'"Here have I drunk fragrant wine,"' she incanted in that sad, slow voice of hers, proceeding out from her in cloudy breaths. '"Sung songs, hunted deer and wild boar. Here have I seen green forests, fields, rivers, lakes, cities. Here have I heard sirens sing and the Pipes of Pan." The Prisoner's message—Chekhov. Do you know it?'

I realized she was talking to me. She had stopped walking and was looking up at me. I blushed. I didn't know it, I said, but I liked her garden.

This seemed to please her. 'Come down and see it properly,' she said, ' But get dressed first. It's still quite chilly.'

I wasn't sure I wanted to see her garden properly—at least not so early—but I also didn't want to get back into that bed, so I dressed, took an old quilted jacket from the back of the door, and went down. A heavy dew had fallen in the night, and the garden was full of scents which hit me as soon as I walked through the door. It was as if the world had been newborn. The birds were singing. The lawn was glittering and wet. The sun was breaking through, and the whole garden was bathed in its light.

Even Miss Chertkova, buried in her coat, shone.

'You could help me if you wanted to,' she said, taking out her gardening gloves and putting them on. 'That's if it won't spoil your nice clothes.'

I could have made it my excuse, and gone back indoors. Mum was very fussy about my church clothes; everything had to be just right for Sunday. But for some reason I didn't. I buttoned up the quilted jacket, and Miss Chertkova went to the shed and brought out her wheelbarrow.

'Well, let's get on with it,' she said.

Up and down between the delphiniums and hollyhocks we trundled, between the roses and herbs and flowering trees, re-tying straggling blooms weighed down with dew, and pulling up weeds. All the while, she told me what things were, and how to look after them.

'A flower like this one wants the sun. These shoots need pruning in the autumn. Plants like these prefer the shade...'

She never smiled, but I could tell that, in her own way, she was pleased to have company. As we passed, she snipped a flower here and a flower there and put them in the wheelbarrow. When it was time to go home, she handed them to me.

'You could give them to your mother,' she said, looking at me with those eyes of hers which gave nothing away. 'Or put them in the church. Whatever you think.'

I thanked her, holding the flowers against myself. It was very kind I was sure, but I wouldn't waste them on church. I hated going to church; it was a kind of prison.

To my surprise, she smiled at me as if she knew what I was thinking. It was only a small smile, but it occurred to me that she didn't look so old after all. I realized I wasn't so frightened of her any more. She was odd, but she was all right.

'You must come again,' she said.

Outside, the snow had turned into a blizzard. I could hardly see through the window-pane, but I could hear undaunted carol singers all the same, coming along the lane from house to house. I drew the curtains and switched on the radio. It was bad enough that the princess had died—but at Christmas time, with its particular memory?

I untied the package, and a scrapbook fell out, bulging with photographs and notes, and newspaper items in English and Russian. ANNA CHERTKOVA, its cover said. The words were worn. I opened the book randomly, turning the pages back and back until something stopped me.

The something was me, staring up from the page. There I was, my own young self, in Indian skirt and hiking boots and baggy jumper, with the words CLUN FOREST, REMEMBER? written under my photograph.

We had been celebrating what we both realized was the end of my old life. In a week's time I'd have gone away to university and the tacit fiendship which had grown up between the princess and me would have faded. I'd remember her as a chapter in my childhood, and no more. I think we both knew how it would be. It was she who suggested the hike, but I remember how important it was to both of us that we got the day right.

It began perfectly enough. Carrying our picnic things we processed beneath a vault of trees, while shafts of sunlight shone through their green-and-yellow leaves, and birds sang hymns. We were very quiet, but that was usual. Miss Chertkova took a photograph of me, and she even let me take one of her, 'for posterity,' as I put it. But then I made some silly joke about growing up, and Miss Chertkova turned on me.

'Growing up's a fearful thing,' she said with passion. 'People think it's about finding themselves. They think it's about discovering what they believe in life, but they've got it wrong. We're born knowing who we are and what we believe. What happens when we grow is that we change ourselves to what other people want us to be.'

Her words were so forceful that they unnerved me. I had never heard her speak like this. It was as if some sort of mask had slipped. I looked away, out of common decency. I didn't understand what she was on about.

She had unnerved herself, too. 'Of course, you're the one who's growing up,' she said, less forcefully. 'You may not agree with me.'

We walked on into a clearing. The sky was still blue above our heads and the grass still green, but everything seemed different somehow. The silence between us was no longer comfortable. Miss Chertkova laid a white cloth on the ground, and I began to talk again, trying to put things back on an easy footing. But she didn't join in; she seemed to have sunk deeply into her own silence. When I looked across at her she was kneeling in front of the tablecloth, her hands shaking, her face flushed.

'Here, let me help you,' I said, hurrying to her side.

She had become preoccupied with putting things in the right place. Bread, cheese, apples, wine—she laid them out, then shook them off the cloth and started again.

'Tell me what's wrong,' I said.

Above our heads, the birds sang and the sun shone and shone. But there were tears in Miss Chertkova's eyes, and I'd never seen her cry before.

'Is it what I said?'

In the end she gave up trying with the picnic things. She folded up the tablecloth and put it away.

'I'm feeling tired,' she said. 'I should never have come. Will you take me back?'

You could see her struggling to hold herself in, but her face was crumbling. It was giving in. 'She's not quite right,' people sometimes said, and I remembered it.

'Don't worry about a thing,' I said. 'I'll take you home.'

'Home,' she said. I never would have thought the word could sound so lonely.

We returned through the forest silently. It was the same day, but everything had changed. I thought how little I knew of Miss Chertkova's past and what might have made her act so strangely.

All the way back, we were silent. Only when we reached her gate, did Miss Chertkova fix me with her eyes and say, in a semblance of her old self, and as if it were an ordinary, cheerful day, 'I hear in the village that you've *met someone*.'

I had been meaning to tell her—not that there was much to say—but I hadn't even hinted at it yet; it hadn't been the right sort of day.

'Yes, I suppose I have,' I said, astonished at the way things got around. 'I know it's a crazy time, what with going off to university, but we can't help these things, can we? He sings in church. He's got a lovely voice. You must come and hear him some time.'

'In church,' said Miss Chertkova, whom I'd never seen in church in all the years I'd known her.

'It's probably nothing, but it could be love,' I said flippantly.

She didn't laugh, just lowered her head. 'Ah, love,' she said.

She came to church the Sunday before Christmas. I was just back from university, and I pleaded with her to come along for no other reason than that I wanted to show off my wonderful boy. I have never forgiven myself for that. I remember waiting for her in the church vestibule, wishing that she would hurry up, and feeling lonely. The place was packed with what felt like the entire festive neighbourhood, greeting each other beneath plastic tinsel and cut-out silver angels and golden stars. A sale had been mounted of religious gifts and Christmas cards, and, in the corner next to the book stall, stood a decorated tree with a box underneath it for donations to the new church window fund.

Only when the service was underway, did I give up waiting and go in. I was disappointed, but there you are. I pushed open the glass doors, and the guitar-and-drum group was up the front, singing before an overhead projector while the congregation tried to keep up with them.

I slid into our family pew and sat down. The vicar and his helpers were handing out decorated oranges with lighted candles in them. By the time they'd finished, the whole, high building with its statues, and stained-glass, and polished brass, seemed to be alive with candlelight.

The guitar group finished their modern song, and the choir rose to sing a traditional one. My boy on the end smiled at me imperceptibly, offering the clear, pure magic of his song. Oh, I wished Miss Chertkova could hear him! I closed my eyes, mesmerized.

All through the service, whatever else went on, I heard the song with only his voice singing it. And at the end when the vicar called on us to impart upon each other a sign of Christmas peace, there was only one person I wanted to kiss.

'Happy Christmas,' I said, when we reached each other in the throng. 'Love, and joy and peace.'

It was the last of love and joy and peace.

Beyond the glass church doors there came a sudden, almighty crash, followed by a thin, high scream and a cascade of tinkling, crunching, and falling down.

At first we froze, the whole lot of us. But then a vase came flying through one of the doors, and a noticeboard through the other one, accompanied by a further scream—and we all turned round.

And there she was, still screaming while all around her cards and gifts rained down. The tree was down, its fairy lights smashed. The decorations were down, all those silver angels and gold stars which had taken so long to put up. The books were down. The glass doors were shattered.

Miss Chertkova.

Even before I saw her, I knew who it would be. I don't know why; some instinct told me. I ran to the broken doors, but she looked straight through me. We might have never met. She stood among the mess she'd made, rending her clothes until they hung in black shreds.

I wanted to weep. How long had she been out there, looking in on us, working herself up to this? I had no idea. The vicar came up behind me. His face was grim. He went through the doors, and Miss Chertkova backed away from him. Her breasts were sticking out of her dress like two wounds.

'Don't be frightened,' he said—and I wondered whose nerves he was steadying, hers or his.

'Get away from me!' she answered him.

By this time, we were all there, peering through the doors at this wild woman with her torn clothes and sticking-up hair who stared back at us, full in all our faces. None of us knew what to do. Icy with contempt,

Miss Chertkova reached into her rags and produced a coin which she inserted in what remained of the collecting box under the tree. Then, with what in the circumstances was extraordinary dignity, she ran out into the night, weeping.

I found the second letter attached to the first. It was just a letter-headed note from the hospital, briefly informing me that the late Anna Chertkova had passed away quietly and, at the end at least, with great clarity of mind.

I remembered her as I'd seen her those few times in the hospital, sitting in a chair in her dressing gown, unable to remember why she was there, singing out in that voice of hers that she didn't know who I was. I was glad she had died, after all these years, with clarity of mind. Glad she had that at least.

I went back to her own letter, and read it properly. The handwriting was shaky, and it took some time, but I worked it all out.

'I owe you an explanation,' it said, as if it had all happened only yesterday. 'You mustn't blame yourself. It's nothing to do with you. It's to do with things that happened long ago.

'Remember me saying that we're born knowing who we are, and what we believe? Well, life was very simple once. I was my parents' child, and we loved God, but we lived in the old Russia—communist Russia, you understand—and we had to do it secretly.

'Every Sunday, my parents used to pack up a picnic lunch and take me on a tram to the outskirts of town. From there we used to walk into the forest, but we weren't nature-lovers out for the day. We were going to church, you see. Our building had been taken from us, and we had to worship secretly.

'When I was seventeen, a foreign delegation visited our town. They were the guests of our government, invited to see for themselves how tolerant our country was towards religious practices. They went from one government-controlled church to another one, and I was outraged. I loved God with my whole heart, and his true priests were in prison, and his true churches closed down and their people driven into the forests.

'I was young, and hot. Before the delegation left, I made a protest. When the foreigners saw it, some of them cried. A lady with tears in her eyes handed me a rose.

'I paid for the action, of course, as we always did. They said that I was sick and took me away. And it was while I was away, in their special prison hospital, that the gesture of the rose and the tears—the easy gesture that cost nothing—came to mean nothing to me too. I grew up, I suppose. Certainly it hurt too much, this loving a God I couldn't see. Perhaps I hadn't loved him after all. Perhaps I didn't even know what love was.

'They let me out of hospital to make a new life. I had become the person they wanted me to be, you see. Even after I came here, there was no returning to my old self. Or so I thought.

'Do you remember Clun Forest? My early days came back to me with such clarity and freshness that it terrified me. And when I went to that cluttered, bustling church of yours, I remembered again how my own people used to worship, and I was overwhelmed by its simplicity. The pure faith; bread and wine beneath the trees. I knew that all that pomp and circumstance of decorations and church window funds could never give you people what

155

we had. *Spirit and truth* we called it, and we didn't pay for it in the box at the door.

'A doctor's just been round to see me. He wanted me to talk about my prison years, but I could never tell him. He wouldn't understand, but I'm telling you. You see, I don't want you to mistake all this trappery for the real thing in which I still—despite everything—believe.

'I inhabited a wilderness all the years you knew me. And now I am a prisoner again. But at least I have my green forests back again, my fields, rivers, lakes, cities. My sirens singing and the Pipes of Pan. Remember?

'It ends as it began. Perhaps I've always been behind bars. And what for this time? For love, I suppose. A fool for love, after all.'

I folded up the letter, and put it in the book. The blizzard howled outside my window. The radio blared. The carol singers' voices rang out. But the only voice I understood was the princess's, inside my head.

'*I was my parents' child, and we loved God, but we lived in Russia and we had to do it secretly...*'

I began to thumb back through her book, past the photographs and sketches, the entries in English and the Russian ones, until I came upon what I knew I'd find, somewhere. A father, and a mother, and a baby on the knee.

Would that it could have been that simple for me, I thought, and anger overwhelmed me. Anger at the tragedy of Miss Chertkova's life. But anger too at what I'd allowed bitterness, or boredom, or distrust—or whatever it had been—to make of mine.

I looked at the snow beating down the window-pane. Somewhere out there, I thought, is a garden full of dustbins and washing lines where once delphiniums grew, and flowering herbs and every sort of rose. The people who own it now don't know what it used to be. But I know. I came as a child to that shining garden. I saw it with my own eyes.

I put away the book, switched off the radio, hung up the black clothes. These thoughts were too high, they were too hard for me; I would think about them later. It was Christmas, after all. Time for greeting cards, and tinsel, and mince-pies.

The Hint of
an Explanation

GRAHAM GREENE

A long train journey on a late December evening, in this new version of peace, is a dreary experience. I suppose that my fellow traveller and I could consider ourselves lucky to have a compartment to ourselves, even though the heating apparatus was not working, even though the lights went out entirely in the frequent Pennine tunnels and were too dim anyway for us to read our books without straining the eyes, and though there was no restaurant car to give at least a change of scene. It was when we were trying simultaneously to chew the same kind of dry bun bought at the same station buffet that my companion and I came together. Before that we had sat at opposite ends of the carriage, both muffled to the chin in overcoats, both bent low over type we could barely make out, but as I threw the remains of my cake under the seat our eyes met, and he laid his book down.

By the time we were half-way to Bedwell Junction we had found an enormous range of subjects for discussion; starting with buns and the weather, we had gone on to politics, the Government, foreign affairs, the atom bomb, and by an inevitable progression, God. We had not, however, become either shrill or acid. My companion, who now sat opposite me, leaning a little forward, so that our knees nearly touched, gave such an impression of serenity that it would have been impossible to quarrel with him, however much our views differed, and differ they did profoundly.

I had soon realized I was speaking to a Roman Catholic—to someone who believed—how do they put it?—in an omnipotent and omniscient Deity, while I am what is loosely called an agnostic. I have a certain intuition (which I do not trust, founded as it may well be on childish experiences and needs) that a God exists, and I am surprised occasionally into belief by the extraordinary coincidences that beset our path like the traps set for leopards in the jungle, but intellectually I am revolted at the whole notion of such a God who can so abandon his creatures to the enormities of Free Will. I found myself expressing this view to my companion who listened quietly and with respect. He made no attempt to interrupt—he showed none of the impatience or the intellectual arrogance I have grown to expect from Catholics; when the lights of a wayside station flashed across this face which had escaped hitherto the rays of the one globe working in the compartment, I caught a glimpse suddenly of—what? I stopped speaking, so strong was the impression. I was carried back ten years, to the other side of the great useless conflict, to a small town, Gisors in Normandy. I was again, for a moment, walking on the ancient battlements and looking down across the grey roofs, until my eyes for some reason lit on one stony 'back' out of the many, where the face of a middle-aged man was pressed against a window pane (I suppose that face has ceased to exist now, just as perhaps the whole town with its medieval memories has been reduced to rubble). I remembered saying to myself with astonishment, 'That man is happy—completely happy.' I looked across the compartment at my fellow traveller, but his face was already again in shadow. I said weakly, 'When you think what God—if there is a God—allows. It's not merely the physical agonies, but think of the corruption, even of children...'

He said, 'Our view is so limited,' and I was disappointed at the conventionality of his reply. He must have been aware of my disappointment (it was as though our thoughts were huddled as closely as ourselves for warmth), for he went on, 'Of course there is no answer here. We catch hints...' and then the train roared into another tunnel and the lights again went out. It was the longest tunnel yet; we went rocking down it and the cold seemed to become more intense with the darkness, like an icy fog (when one sense—of sight—is robbed, the others grow more acute). When we emerged into the mere grey of night and the globe lit up once more, I could see that my companion was leaning back on his seat.

I repeated his last word as a question, 'Hints?'

'Oh, they mean very little in cold print—or cold speech,' he said, shivering in his overcoat. 'And they mean nothing at all to another human being than the man who catches them. They are not scientific evidence—or evidence at all for that matter. Events that don't, somehow, turn out as they were intended—by the human actors, I mean, or by the thing behind the human actors.'

'The thing?'

'The word Satan is so anthropomorphic.' I had to lean forward now: I wanted to hear what he had to say. I am—I really am, God knows—open to conviction. He said, 'One's words are so crude, but I sometimes feel pity for that thing. It is so continually finding the right weapon to use against its Enemy and the weapon breaks in its own breast. It sometimes seems to me so—powerless. You said something just now about the corruption of children. It reminded me of something in my own childhood. You are the first person—except for one—that I have thought of telling it to, perhaps because you are anonymous. It's not a very long story, and in a way it's relevant.'

I said, 'I'd like to hear it.'

'You mustn't expect too much meaning. But to me there seems to be a hint. That's all. A hint.'

He went slowly on turning his face to the pane, though he could have seen nothing in the whirling world outside except an occasional signal lamp, a light in a window, a small country station torn backwards by our rush, picking his words with precision. He said, 'When I was a child they taught me to serve at Mass. The church was a small one, for there were very few Catholics where I lived. It was a market town in East Anglia, surrounded by flat chalky fields and ditches—so many ditches. I don't suppose there were fifty Catholics all told, and for some reason there was a tradition of hostility to us. Perhaps it went back to the burning of a Protestant martyr in the sixteenth century—there was a stone marking the place near where the meat stalls stood on Wednesdays. I was only half aware of the enmity, though I knew that my school nickname of Popey Martin had something to do with my religion and I had heard that my father was very nearly excluded from the Constitutional Club when he first came to the town.

'Every Sunday I had to dress up in my surplice and serve Mass. I hated it—I have always hated dressing up in any way (which is funny when you come to think of it), and I never ceased to be afraid of losing my place in the service and doing something which would put me to ridicule. Our services were at a different hour from the Anglican, and as our small, far-from-select band trudged out of the hideous chapel the whole of the townsfolk seemed to be on the way past to the proper church—I always thought of it as the proper church. We had to pass the parade of their eyes, indifferent, supercilious, mocking; you can't imagine how seriously religion can be taken in a small town—if only for social reasons.

'There was one man in particular; he was one of the two bakers in the town, the one my family did not patronize. I don't think any of the Catholics patronized him because he was called a free-thinker—an odd title, for, poor man, no one's thoughts were less free than his. He was hemmed in by his hatred—his hatred of us. He was very ugly to look at, with one wall-eye and a head the shape of a turnip, with the hair gone on the crown, and he was unmarried. He had no interests, apparently, but his baking and his hatred, though now that I am older I begin to see other sides of his nature—it did contain, perhaps, a certain furtive love. One would come across him suddenly, sometimes, on a country walk, especially if one was alone and it was Sunday. It was as though he rose from the ditches and the chalk smear on his clothes reminded one of the flour on his working overalls. He would have a stick in his hand and stab at the hedges, and if his mood were very black he would call out after you strange abrupt words that were like a foreign tongue—I know the meaning of those words, of course, now. Once the police went to his house because of what a boy said he had seen, but nothing came of it except that the hate shackled him closer. His name was Blacker, and he terrified me.

'I think he had a particular hatred of my father—I don't know why. My father was manager of the Midland Bank, and it's possible that at some time Blacker may have had unsatisfactory dealings with the bank—my father was a very cautious man who suffered all his life from anxiety about money—his own and other people's. If I try to picture Blacker now I see him walking along a narrowing path between high windowless walls, and at the end of the path stands a small boy of ten—me. I don't know whether it's a symbolic picture or the memory of one of our encounters—our encounters somehow got more and more frequent. You talked just now about the corruption of children. That poor man was preparing to revenge himself on everything he hated—my father, the Catholics, the God whom people persisted in crediting—by corrupting me. He had evolved a horrible and ingenious plan.

'I remember the first time I had a friendly word from him. I was passing his shop as rapidly as I could when I heard his voice call out with a kind of sly subservience as though he were an under-servant. 'Master David,' he called, 'Master David,' and I hurried on. But the next time I passed that way he was at his door (he must have seen me coming) with one of those curly cakes in his hand that we called Chelsea buns. I didn't want to take it, but he made me, and then I couldn't be other than polite when he asked me to come into his parlour behind the shop and see something very special.

'It was a small electric railway—a rare sight in those days, and he insisted on showing me how it worked. He made me turn the switches and stop and start it, and he told me that I could come in any morning and have a game with it. He used the word "game" as though it were something secret, and it's true that I never told my family of this invitation and of how, perhaps twice a week those holidays, the desire to control that little railway became overpowering, and looking up and down the street to see if I were observed, I would dive into the shop.'

Our larger, dirtier, adult train drove into a tunnel and the light went out. We sat in darkness and silence, with the noise of the train blocking our ears like wax. When we were through we didn't speak at once and I had to prick him into continuing.

'An elaborate seduction,' I said.

'Don't think his plans were as simple as that,' my companion said, 'or as crude. There was much more hate than love, poor man, in his make-up. Can you hate something you don't believe in? And yet he called himself a free-thinker. What an impossible paradox, to be free and to be so obsessed. Day by day all through those holidays his obsession must have grown, but he kept a grip; he bided his time. Perhaps that thing I spoke of gave him the strength and the wisdom. It was only a week from the end of the holidays that he spoke to me of what concerned him so deeply.

'I heard him behind me as I knelt on the floor, coupling

two coaches. He said, "You won't be able to do this, Master David, when school starts." It wasn't a sentence that needed any comment from me any more than the one that followed, "You ought to have it for your own, you ought," but how skilfully and unemphatically he had sowed the longing, the idea of a possibility... I was coming to his parlour every day now; you see I had to cram every opportunity in before the hated term started again, and I suppose I was becoming accustomed to Blacker, to that wall-eye, that turnip head, that nau-seating subservience. The Pope, you know, describes himself as "The servant of the servant of God", and Blacker—I sometimes think, that Blacker was "the servant of the servants of..." well, let it be.

'The very next day, standing in the doorway watching me play, he began to talk to me about religion. He said, with what untruth even I recognized, how much he admired the Catholics; he wished he could believe like that, but how could a baker believe? He accented "a baker" as one might say a biologist, and the tiny train spun round the gauge-O track. He said, "I can bake the things you eat just as well as any Catholic can," and disappeared into his shop. I hadn't the faintest idea what he meant. Presently he emerged again, holding in his hand a little wafer. "Here," he said, "eat that and tell me..." When I put it in my mouth I could tell that it was made in the same way as our wafers for communion—he had got the shape a little wrong, that was all, and I felt guilty and irrationally scared. "Tell me," he said, "what's the difference?"

'"Difference?" I asked.

'"Isn't that just the same as you eat in church?"

'I said smugly, "It hasn't been consecrated."

'He said, "Do you think if I put the two of them under a microscope, you could tell the difference?" But even at ten I had the answer to that question. "No," I said, "the—accidents don't change," stumbling a little on the word "accidents" which had suddenly conveyed to me the idea of death and wounds.

'Blacker said with sudden intensity, "How I'd like to get one of yours in my mouth—just to see..."

'It may seem odd to you, but this was the first time that the idea of transubstantiation really lodged in my mind. I had learnt it all by rote; I had grown up with the idea. The Mass was as lifeless to me as the sentences in *De Bello Gallico*, communion a routine like drill in the school-yard, but here suddenly I was in the presence of a man who took it seriously, as seriously as the priest whom naturally one didn't count—it was his job. I felt more scared than ever.

'He said, "It's all nonsense, but I'd just like to have it in my mouth."

'"You could if you were a Catholic," I said naively. He gazed at me with his one good eye like a Cyclops. He said, "You serve at Mass, don't you? It would be easy for you to get at one of those things. I tell you what I'd do—I'd swap this electric train set for one of your wafers—consecrated, mind. It's got to be consecrated."

'"I could get you one out of the box," I said. I think I still imagined that his interest was a baker's interest—to see how they were made.

'"Oh, no," he said. "I want to see what your God tastes like."

'"I couldn't do that."

'"Not for a whole electric train, just for yourself? You wouldn't have any trouble at home. I'd pack it up and

166

put a label inside that your Dad could see—"For my bank manager's little boy from a grateful client." He'd be pleased as Punch with that."

'Now that we are grown men it seems a trivial temptation, doesn't it? But try to think back to your own childhood. There was a whole circuit of rails on the floor at our feet, straight rails and curved rails, and a little station with porters and passengers, a tunnel, a foot-bridge, a level crossing, two signals, buffers, of course—and above all, a turntable. The tears of longing came into my eyes when I looked at the turntable. It was my favourite piece—it looked so ugly and practical and true. I said weakly, "I wouldn't know how."

'How carefully he had been studying the ground. He must have slipped several times into Mass at the back of the church. It would have been no good, you understand, in a little town like that, presenting himself for com-munion. Everybody there knew him for what he was. He said to me, "When you've been given communion you could just put it under your tongue a moment. He serves you and the other boy first, and I saw you once go out behind the curtain straight afterwards. You'd forgotten one of those little bottles."

'"The cruet," I said.

'"Pepper and salt." He grinned at me jovially, and I—well, I looked at the little railway which I could no longer come and play with when term started. I said, "You'd just swallow it, wouldn't you?"

'"Oh, yes," he said, "I'd just swallow it."

'Somehow I didn't want to play with the train any more that day. I got up and made for the door, but he detained me, gripping my lapel. He said, "This will be a secret between you and me. Tomorrow's Sunday. You come along here in the afternoon. Put it in an envelope and post it in. Monday morning the train will be delivered bright and early."

'"Not tomorrow," I implored him.

'"I'm not interested in any other Sunday," he said. "It's your only chance." He shook me gently backwards and forwards. "It will always have to be a secret between you and me," he said. "Why, if anyone knew they'd take away the train and there'd be me to reckon with. I'd bleed you something awful. You know how I'm always about on Sunday walks. You can't avoid a man like me. I crop up. You wouldn't even be safe in your own house. I know ways to get into houses when people are asleep." He pulled me into the shop after him and opened a drawer. In the drawer was an odd-looking key and a cut-throat razor. He said, "That's a master key that opens all locks and that—that's what I bleed people with." Then he patted my cheek with his plump floury fingers and said, "Forget it. You and me are friends."

'That Sunday Mass stays in my head, every detail of it, as though it had happened only a week ago. From the moment of the Confession to the moment of Consecration it had a terrible importance; only one other Mass has ever been so important to me—perhaps not even one, for this was a solitary Mass which could never happen again. It seemed as final as the last Sacrament, when the priest bent down and put the wafer in my mouth where I knelt before the altar with my fellow server.

'I suppose I had made up my mind to commit this awful act—for, you know, to us it must always seem an awful act—from the moment when I saw Blacker watching from the back of the church. He had put on his best Sunday clothes, and as though he could never quite escape the smear of his profession, he had a dab of dried talcum on his cheek, which he had presumably applied after using that cut-throat of his. He was watching me closely all the time, and I think it was fear—fear of that terrible undefined thing called bleeding—as much as covetousness that drove me to carry out my instructions.

'My fellow server got briskly up and taking the communion plate preceded Father Carey to the altar rail where the other Communicants knelt. I had the Host lodged under my tongue: it felt like a blister. I got up and made for the curtain to get the cruet that I had purposely left in the sacristy. When I was there I looked quickly round for a hiding-place and saw an old copy of the *Universe* lying on a chair. I took the Host from my mouth and inserted it between two sheets—a little damp mess of pulp. Then I thought: perhaps Father Carey has put the paper out for a particular purpose and he will find the Host before I have time to remove it, and the enormity of my act began to come home to me when I tried to imagine what punishment I should incur. Murder is sufficiently trivial to have its appropriate punishment, but for this act the mind boggled at the thought of any retribution at all. I tried to remove the Host, but it had stuck clammily between the pages and in desperation I tore out a piece of the newspaper and, screwing the whole thing up, stuck it in my trouser pocket. When I came back through the curtain carrying the cruet my eyes met Blacker's. He gave me a grin of encouragement and unhappiness—yes, I am sure, unhappiness. Was it perhaps that the poor man was all the time seeking something incorruptible?

'I can remember little more of that day. I think my mind was shocked and stunned and I was caught up too in the family bustle of Sunday. Sunday in a provincial town is the day for relations. All the family are at home and unfamiliar cousins and uncles are apt to arrive packed in the back seats of other people's cars. I remember that some crowd of that kind descended on us and pushed Blacker temporarily out of the foreground of my mind. There was somebody called Aunt Lucy with a loud hollow laugh that filled the house with mechanical merriment like the sound of recorded laughter from inside a hall of mirrors, and I had no opportunity to go out alone even if I had wished to. When six o'clock came and Aunt Lucy and the cousins departed and peace returned, it was too late to go to Blacker's and at eight it was my own bed-time.

'I think I had half forgotten what I had in my pocket. As I emptied my pocket the little screw of newspaper brought quickly back the Mass, the priest bending over me, Blacker's grin. I laid the packet on the chair by my bed and tried to go to sleep, but I was haunted by the shadows on the wall where the curtains blew, the squeak of furniture, the rustle in the chimney, haunted by the presence of God there on the chair. The Host had always been to me—well, the Host. I knew theoretically, as I have said, what I had to believe, but suddenly, as someone whistled in the road outside, whistled secretively, knowingly, to me, I knew that this which I had beside my bed was something of infinite value—something a man would pay for with his whole peace of mind, something that was so hated one could love it as one loves an outcast or a bullied child. These are adult words and it was a child of ten who lay scared in bed, listening to the whistle from the road, Blacker's whistle, but I think he felt fairly clearly what I am describing now. That is what I meant when I said this Thing, whatever it is, that seizes every possible weapon against God, is always, everywhere, disappointed at the moment of success. It must have felt as certain of me as Blacker did. It must have felt certain, too, of Blacker. But I wonder, if one knew what happened later to that poor man, whether one would not find again that the weapon had been turned against its own breast.

'At last I couldn't bear that whistle any more and got out of bed. I opened the curtains a little way, and there right under my window, the moonlight on his face, was Blacker. If I had stretched my hand down, his fingers reaching up could almost have touched mine. He looked up at me, flashing the one good eye, with hunger—I realize now that near-success must have developed his obsession almost to the point of madness. Desperation had driven him to the house. He whispered up at me, "David, where is it?"

'I jerked my head back at the room. "Give it me," he said, "quick. You shall have the train in the morning."

'I shook my head. He said, "I've got the bleeder here, and the key. You'd better toss it down."

' "Go away," I said, but I could hardly speak with fear.

' "I'll bleed you first and then I'll have it just the same."

' "Oh no, you won't," I said. I went to the chair and picked it—Him—up. There was only one place where He was safe. I couldn't separate the Host from the paper, so I swallowed both. The newsprint stuck like a prune to the back of my throat, but I rinsed it down with water from the ewer. Then I went back to the window and looked down at Blacker. He began to wheedle me. "What have you done with it, David? What's the fuss? It's only a bit of bread," looking so longingly and pleadingly up at me that even as a child I wondered whether he could really think that, and yet desire it so much.

'"I swallowed it," I said.

'"Swallowed it?"

'"Yes," I said. "Go away." Then something happened which seems to me now more terrible than his desire to corrupt or my thoughtless act: he began to weep—the tears ran lopsidedly out of the one good eye and his shoulders shook. I only saw his face for a moment before he bent his head and strode off, the bald turnip head shaking, into the dark. When I think of it now, it's almost as if I had seen that Thing weeping for its inevitable defeat. It had tried to use me as a weapon and now I had broken in its hands and it wept its hopeless tears through one of Blacker's eyes.'

The black furnaces of Bedwell Junction gathered around the line. The points switched and we were tossed from one set of rails to another. A spray of sparks, a signal light changed to red, tall chimneys jetting into the grey night sky, the fumes of steam from stationary engines—half the cold journey was over and now remained the long wait for the slow cross-country train. I said, 'It's an interesting story. I think I should have given Blacker what he wanted. I wonder what he would have done with it.'

'I really believe,' my companion said, 'that he would first of all have put it under his microscope—before he did all the other things I expect he had planned.'

'And the hint?' I said. 'I don't quite see what you mean by that.'

'Oh, well,' he said vaguely, 'you know for me it was an odd beginning, that affair, when you come to think of it,' but I should never have known what he meant had not his coat, when he rose to take his bag from the rack, come open and disclosed the collar of a priest.

I said, 'I suppose you think you owe a lot to Blacker.'

'Yes,' he said. 'You see, I am a very happy man.'

Towards the
Unknown Region

A N N   P I L L I N G

I have just said goodbye to an old friend. It was my own decision, an act of my conscious will. But I am not sure, now, that I should have done such a thing because I find that I am in mourning. In the deep hours of night when the house, having grown tall, threatens to tumble down, to compress itself and crush me, I scream aloud, wanting the comfort of my friend.

I blame this unhappiness on my last birthday, the birthday on which I became fifty years old. On that day it came to me that I must enter into a new phase of my life, that I must simplify my existence and try to walk more closely with the Lord our God. Part of my new walk was to be that I would honour his creation. From that day forth I would waste nothing.

On the day I got up very early and rang Margery Elliott. She doesn't mind what time I phone her, she's my friend, we went to school together. She started off as a deacon in the Church of England but they've made her into a real priest now. She can do bread and wine and forgive people's sins. She understands more than I do, I mean about God's things.

'Marge,' I said, when she picked up the phone, 'Hiya, it's my birthday. From this day forth I want to honour the Lord's creation. Tell me what I must do.'

Straight away she said 'Happy Birthday', but after that there was a little pause. Then she said 'Are you all right, Miriam? It's awfully early. I'd not forgotten today was the day, only I have to do hospital visiting this morning. I was planning to drop in later. But if you need me—'

I said 'I'm OK, Marge, I'm not panicking. You don't have to come round. I just want to get on.'

'What with, love?' Marge sounded puzzled. 'It's only six o'clock.'

'With God's creation. Tell me what to do. I've got a pencil.'

Marge hesitated again, then she began to speak, very slowly and carefully; you can tell she used to be a teacher. I wrote everything down and when she'd rung off I read it through.

It involved the acquisition of some cardboard cartons, 'stout' cartons Marge had advised. I very much like the word 'stout'. 'Take a stout cigar box' it said in *One Hundred Things a Boy Can Make* and I so wanted a cigar box, to make a little guitar. All through the years I waited tremulously for my father or one of his friends to give me one. There were certainly cigars at Christmas time but no box ever came down to me. My brother always seemed to get them and he crammed them full with oily foreign coins, my little brother who is dead.

I had a bath and got dressed. Then I fed Geoffrey and ate a bowl of muesli. When I'd washed up (there were three days of dishes but who cares? It's one of the perks of living alone) I got my car out and drove to the supermarket on the edge of town. It was Monday and the aisles were almost empty. On Friday nights, the time I usually do my shopping, the competition for cardboard boxes can be ferocious but that morning I had them all to myself, a whole stack of them, really marvellous cartons, perfectly clean and quite undamaged, cartons of every possible size. I loaded up the boot of the car feeling quite light-headed.

When I got home I put them in the garage, having first made sure there were no patches of oil on the floor. I didn't want to dirty the boxes, it was part of my new walk, not to be messy any more. There wasn't any oil because I never bother to put my car away. Richard, my ex-husband, always did, but of course his car did not leak, not ever. My sluttish attitude towards the well-being of our cars annoyed him. It is better that he has gone; we could no longer make one another happy.

When I opened the kitchen door Geoffrey, my two-year-old, leapt into my arms. We have always had cats though I had to do battle with Richard to get one, when we were first married. He has no feelings for animals. I can't remember how many cats I've had so far, six or seven, there has been the usual wastage. I've loved them all but there has never been a cat like Geoffrey. He is not beautiful, pale ginger, the colour of a well-baked biscuit, but with too small a head and a fat little tail. 'Plume Cat' I sometimes call him. Richard said that Geoffrey was a stupid name, a name for a schoolboy, not a name for cats. But Geoffrey was the cat who belonged to the mad poet

Christopher Smart. (Poetry's another thing Richard has no time for.) 'I will consider my cat Jeoffry,' he wrote. It's a beautiful little poem.

Did you read about that man who shot himself because he'd not won the National Lottery? Someone had hoaxed him and told him he'd won half a million pounds. He was in terrible debt at the time so it was a real miracle, the answer to all his problems. That man was my brother Michael. I know what Richard would have said. 'I'm not really surprised. Your family was always mad.' He had no time for Michael and his troubles, he despised weakness in people. The shooting happened after he'd left me for Crystal and he never contacted me about it, not a word.

I now think that things started to break down after we got Geoffrey. Richard was jealous of him. 'You love that cat more than you love me' he said, and I answered 'Well, he gives *me* love. You don't.'

'Animals cannot feel love,' he argued back (he has always enjoyed putting me down). 'Love is a human emotion. Animals have no capacity for love, and no sense of duty if it comes to that. They have no moral sense either. Any thought that they might have these things comes from you. It's called anthropomorphism.'

'Well he's purring,' I said, 'Why should he do that, when he's just been fed? Don't tell me it's cupboard love.'

'Purring doesn't mean happiness. Purring is merely to humour you, so you'll be conned into giving him more food.'

'Well I love him,' I said 'And he loves me. Furthermore he'd love me whatever I do to him. He's about God.'

'You are mad,' Richard said coldly, slipping the rubber bands off that morning's post. It was the day he stuffed a blue envelope into his pocket unopened. He thought I'd not noticed but he'd put it away so fast he'd crushed it. So I investigated later and discovered that it was the first letter from Crystal. She'd been ultra-cautious up till then.

I put Geoffrey on the floor and plugged in the kettle for some coffee. I didn't want coffee, I wanted a drink, but I was trying to be good. 'No point in getting help then turning your back on it, is it?' I said to him. He jumped up again so I settled him into my hip joint, to carry him around. Once I carried the babies round like that because, like Geoffrey, they did not want to be separated from their mother. I learned to do everything with one hand, chop onions, load the washing machine, answer the phone. My left hip became quite pronounced, sticking out like a deformity. I can't see my hips any more, they've got lost, buried along with my waist beneath three stones of fat. I *am* going to diet, it's going to be part of my new life, but I can't tackle everything at once. 'Eat your elephant in little bites.' That's what Marge says. Geoffrey purred as I poured hot water on the Nescafe and reached out a paw to grab at the flex. Once I carried my children round the house. These days I carry the cat.

I spent my birthday morning filling up the boxes, with bottles mainly, most of them green. That's because I prefer red wine to white. A Rioja suits me very well, it has what they call a big 'shout'. Richard said I had no palate. He is very serious about wine. It was in a wine store that he met Crystal. She was just the woman behind the counter but she obviously knew about wine too, and they got talking. They got pally over a new malt whisky called Sheep Dip. It *was* called that, truly.

This is a large house and it took me a long time to assemble the bottles because I'd put them all over the place, and there are so many rooms. I got a bit frantic, like a hungry squirrel trying to find his store of nuts, but in the end the job was finished and I stood looking at five stout cartons of bottles, mainly green glass but a few white and brown. Those olive oil bottles with leaves round the neck are pretty. I use nothing but olive oil these days because it's so good for us. That was another clue about Richard and Crystal. He started not turning up for meals and he'd always enjoyed his food. (I'm a good cook; everybody says so.)

I humped all the bottles into the boot of my car, all five boxes, then a sixth which was full of rags. Marge had explained that there's a rag bank and a paper bank. There's a bank for tin cans too. Absolutely nothing that God provides for us needs to be wasted. It's marvellous.

Actually, they weren't really 'rags'. There were some old dust-sheets covered with paint that I didn't think I'd ever use again. My days of home decorating are over; life's too short. There was that enormous Norwegian sweater of Nick's that had the big burn hole in it and, folded on top, there was my old brown coat. I'd hesitated over this; it had been such a good friend to me, that coat. But I thought, it's like the painting sheets, I'm never going to use it again. Let it go, Miriam. Don't cling to the past.

Our town is really very conveniently arranged. There's this excellent supermarket just beyond the ring-road and then, only a couple of roads away, a new sports complex with a swimming pool called the Dolphin Centre. Marge swims there every morning at half past six. I'm a very good swimmer, I will say that for myself, and when she first started Marge badgered me to go with her. But I only did it once. It's a lovely pool, well it's brand new of course, but there are no private cubicles to change in, you just have to walk round naked. I couldn't bear it. I don't want to be naked with people any more, not even with Marge whom I have known since we were five years old. I never went again.

There's a car park adjoining the Dolphin Centre and all the banks for household waste are in one corner. It's a 'Pay and Display' system but you don't have to pay if you're only bringing rubbish to get rid of. I personally don't think anyone should have to pay. They've not laid a hard surface yet and it's full of craters. After heavy rainfall it turns into a series of lakes. Last Monday there were seagulls scudding about on the water. I watched them for a while because there was a man chucking things into the waste banks and I felt nervous. It's very exposed that rutted carpark, it backs onto open fields and a biting wind swept over it, sending up a fine gravel that pitted the surface of the little pools. Then the wind took firm hold of the water, frilling it like a choirboy's ruff. It was really pretty but very cold and the man was taking ages.

When he had driven away I advanced in my car and unloaded the boot. The waste banks were simply big metal humps with a series of holes into which you chucked your rubbish and each was clearly labelled in white stencilled letters. The bottle banks were painted green, white and brown and it was all very orderly with a huge wire basket provided for your empty boxes. But I knew that my stout cartons were going to travel home with me; we had started a relationship.

It took me some minutes to get the hang of posting the bottles through the holes. The first few times I missed altogether and they ended up on the gravel. Fortunately the rain and people's feet had made a soft mud otherwise they would have broken. I realized that I must hold them by the neck end, that way I could aim straight. I had maximum control of the bottle and the fat end helped to weigh its descent into the bank. As I neatly posted each bottle I could hear Richard behind me telling me that I was a fool, that all I'd discovered was an elementary physical law. He loved putting me down.

I'd disposed of a whole box of green bottles before I realized that I'd been trying not to break them, and so far I think I had succeeded. This suddenly struck me as ridiculous. The glass was to be recycled and that meant melted down. Breaking the bottles therefore would be a help to the disposal people. So I stood on tiptoes—I'm very short and now I am fat my shape is somewhat gro-tesque, as Richard kindly told me the day we parted—and peered into one of the holes. The floor of the bin was deep in broken glass, the only intact bottles being the ones I had just posted.

I changed my tactics then and started hurling them home with great force, and I began to experience an unexpected pleasure, something mildly orgasmic, as my strong arm movement climaxed in the tinny crash and dismemberment of the glass inside the bin, but more, together with the physical relief, I felt a miraculous letting go, a space opening up inside my head. Down inside the bottle bank I saw Richard's head quite clearly and, in particular, his unkind, curling lips, down there amongst all the broken glass, while I, Miriam, system-atically smashed him out of existence, putting away from me for ever and ever the cruelty and the insults, the desertion. With these things too went all the inadequate feelings, the sense of hopelessness, the daily apologies for being Miriam. I knew, as I hurled my very last bottle, that none of this could ever touch me again. From these ashes I would rise. When I walked away from the curious green humps it felt like floating.

The rag bank was striped cheery yellow and black. Someone on the council had clearly expressed himself and the hole for the rags was a long slit, like a mouth. The same artist had painted pointed teeth below it. I posted through the mouth first my painting sheets then Nick's Norwegian sweater with the big hole burned into it. He did that at someone's party and Richard got furious and blamed me. Nick had been at a barbecue and had leaned against something hot. It was I Richard shouted at, for not going with him. He said, 'You know how scatty those people are. You should never have sent him off alone, to such a family.' But Nicholas had been very much a clinging child, I had wanted to encourage a little independence in him. I was blamed also for having bought such a very expensive sweater and I remembered that, for the very first time, I did not argue, opening my mouth only to say I was sorry. That was definitely the beginning of the break. It was nothing to do with loving Geoffrey.

My very last piece of waste was the old brown coat which I had kept back till the end. I now unfolded it carefully and shook it out; then I examined it. There's a lot of grey in my hair these days and it seemed to me that the coat too had quietly grown old. At its double edges, collar, cuffs and hem, the brown had whitened, like the muzzle of an ancient dog. It had been a soft coat once, a good coat. When the children were still only toddling I had made a special expedition to Oxford to buy it. We lived in the country in those days and this was my first shopping trip alone, to choose something for myself, since

Isabel was born. Gerda had looked after the children and given them tea—she is my most special friend, after Marge. She was living in a cottage outside Henley when I bought the brown coat but after her first stroke the family moved her down to Devon where they all have houses. She is in a home now and I've not seen her for nearly a year. I just can't get down there, it's too far, and there's been all this unhappiness with Richard. She used to write me the most marvellous letters but they stopped after the second stroke. I suppose *I* could write.

Gerda would say that I'd bought a good-tempered coat, that was her word for reassuring, comfortable garments that wrap themselves round you like a lover or a child, 'good-tempered'. She herself had such a coat, a Jaeger coat, a coat the colour of crushed strawberries. I really loved it. She laughed at me once and said 'I might leave it to you in my will.' I expect it's long since been fed into a toothy mouth like this one. Her nephew, the relative who organized the home in Devon, struck me as a bustling, tight individual, exceedingly efficient. He would have reasoned that she would not need her strawberry-coloured coat, where she was going.

What she did give me, when they sold her cottage near Henley, was a small Persian carpet, a prayer rug covered with animals and birds all springing exquisitely from the Tree of Life. I'd always admired that rug. She had said, 'Put it on the floor dear, that's what it's for.' But I hung it on a wall so that we could all see it; it was so beautiful.

When Michael had his troubles I sold the rug and gave him the money. I wish I hadn't now. It had been very clumsily repaired years before and they didn't give me all that much for it. Michael died in any case. Why didn't I keep it?

So the friend I parted with on my birthday morning was my old brown coat. I had to do it quickly in the end, without too much thinking. I stuffed it into the smiling mouth and walked quickly away and the rug, and all it had meant to me, somehow went with it. These are only things, I told myself, they are only fabric, the wrong repositories for memory and absolutely the wrong repositories for hope. I felt light again when I climbed into the car, even lighter than when I'd posted the last of my bottles.

The postman had left my letters in the front porch, quite a thick bundle secured by two rubber bands. I decided I would start saving these and, when I had a goodly number, return them to the post office for re-use. I would look for a tin to store them in that very minute, before I got down to my letters. It would be part of my new walk. In the bundle I could see what looked like cards but not who had sent what because I wasn't wearing my glasses. I didn't open anything. I had the whole day ahead and nobody was going to come and see me except, perhaps, Marge, but I did flatten the envelopes. I do wish they wouldn't do up the post with those rubber bands, it ruins it. There is such joy in a perfectly flat white envelope.

I sat down at the kitchen table thinking, It's my birthday and I've lived for one half of a hundred years. Then I made myself a gin and tonic and sat there peacefully, looking out across the garden. The cat flap rattled and Geoffrey rushed in and leapt onto my knee. He always bursts through his flap like an explosion. I got up, still holding on to him, and found him a bit of cheese. He loves it. I'm trying to break him of the snacking habit (along with myself) but it was my birthday. He tried my gin and tonic after I'd refreshed it but it only made him sneeze.

Then I sat thinking about my visit to the bottle banks and about my old brown coat. It was May when I did that trip to Oxford but a good time to buy a warm coat, Gerda had advised me, fashions always working at least six months ahead. I had left the children with her in her garden where she made up little games for them and gave them 'jobs', watering and pulling out carefully selected weeds. Isabel talked of that day for many years, of the tea she made for them, of the big flat syrup biscuits, of the toy theatre she had cut out of a book for them, with puppets on lollipop sticks.

I remembered the day she last walked on two legs. She had come to have lunch with us and afterwards I went with her to her car. We had moved to the town and she had been obliged to park several streets away, in a side road where you did not have to buy a ticket. Gerda was careful with her money. She bought oriental rugs and fine editions of nineteenth-century poets but she very much begrudged parking fees. That day the wind blew through her thick grey hair wrapping the silk scarf she wore tightly around her neck. Gerda wore her scarves so prettily, in a way I have never been able to imitate. She was wearing her strawberry-coloured coat.

The day afterwards, when the hospital rang, I had to take Nicholas with me. He was only three. They had propped her upright in a chair by her bed, in a white wrap, and her head was bandaged. She had fallen, when the stroke happened. She did not move and she did not speak so we just sat with her for a while, Nicholas on my knee staring up at his Gerda. 'I realize, of course, that

Gerda is an educated woman,' said the nurse. 'When she came round she believed she was in Hell.' After this time, whenever her name was spoken, Nicholas turned his face to the wall.

Gerda, and her good-tempered coat. The old brown coat I had just thrown away was good-tempered also. It had absorbed music, folded on my lap in an Oxford college chapel while a small choir sang *Messiah*. When he heard 'Worthy is the Lamb' Nicholas began to cry. When it had grown too shabby for concerts it became the coat I tramped in. It accompanied us on our biggest-log-in-the-world walk, so exciting, deep, deep into beech woods, jumping over fallen trees, the jumps getting higher and higher until at last one jump was just too high and the children had to be helped up and over. Then, after the biggest log in the world, a little clearing where, mysteriously, an ancient steam-roller stood alone. The children always worried lest this magical thing should have vanished. But, ah, their little bird cries of relief and wonder when, once again, they saw it standing quiet and dignified in the drifting beech mast. In the end my own brown coat became my gardening coat. I dug in it, and stirred bonfires. The smell of autumn was in that coat, and of the woods, and of baby, all my life.

Suddenly I wanted it back. I wished I'd not stuffed it through that slit. I wanted to put my face against it and to breath in what Gerda would have called its 'being', to hear again, through its threads, the choirboys singing Handel. That joy could be mine again and I had thrown it away. It was a churlish action towards such an old friend.

The last time I saw Gerda she spoke about dying. She suddenly said 'When I die, Miriam, I want it to be different from this.' I said 'How "different", Gerda?' She grew thoughtful then, and it seemed that she was trying to find some words. After the first stroke she learned to speak again, after a fashion, but now words float past her like leaves on a river. Sometimes she is able to reach forwards and pluck them out but there is not always a pattern. 'It has left me,' she whispers sadly. She said finally, in answer to my question about death being different, 'I don't know,' with the blankness of someone trying in vain to understand some vast mystery.

When I left her that day I kissed her face. Now I have hardly ever kissed Gerda, she is not a person who touches you. But my kiss awakened something because she started to cry and, with her good hand, touched my cheek. She has become so much softer. I think it must be the approach of death. Our ancient tabby, the cat we had before Geoffrey, was always a shrewish, unfriendly creature but she became most loving in the end, letting us take her on our knee. She seemed at last to need us.

I made myself another gin. It was a big one but it emptied the bottle and I vowed there and then that I would not buy another. Before starting on my very last birthday drink I took the bottle to the carton I had assigned for it, next to the freezer. I would not need to visit the Dolphin Centre for some time because there would be very few bottles, unless I entertained someone and there's nobody much around here these days. A lot of the people we knew have bought smaller houses, now that their children have gone, and have moved away. My house stood empty and neat. At half past four nobody would come tumbling through the door and strew the debris of school across the kitchen, decant cornflakes into a bowl and pour a whole pint of milk on. It would be better to move away.

I picked up my letters and looked through them. There was nothing from Nicholas but I would not expect anything yet. He has only been in India for a month and anyway, he's a boy. 'There is nothing quite like a small boy,' Gerda observed one day, watching him in her garden very seriously occupied with some dirt. She called these mysterious activities his 'ploys'. Isabel had sent a card with a yellow duck on. It was not a birthday card, it merely informed me that the baby had cut another tooth. Shall I ever see this baby? I wondered. I cannot afford to go to Alabama.

Richard had already visited twice, with his new wife Crystal. I am glad my mother called me Miriam, it has some magnificence. *O give thanks unto the Lord, for he hath triumphed gloriously,* Miriam sang. *The horse and his rider hath he thrown into the sea.* 'Crystal'. Where is the history in that? She's having a baby too. Isabel's baby will be its aunt, Isabel its half-sister. We called Isabel Gerda but when she went to university she changed it. She said that Gerda was an ugly, lumpy name.

I did not tell my old friend. She is travelling towards the unknown region but I know that she can still feel pain because, whenever I take my leave of her, when I have reached the door, she turns her face away and weeps. I wish sometimes I could be on that journey too. My house has become so empty. I longed once for quiet, calm days but now they have come I no longer know what to do with them. I don't understand what I'm for.

There was no card from Richard. He would not have forgotten my birthday, he was always very organized. No, he had chosen not to acknowledge it any more because the life we had together is absolutely finished. There was one more item, a long typed envelope which had been posted in Crediton, a fat envelope uncrushed, the kind that gives me joy. I slit it open with the cheese knife and gave it to Geoffrey. He likes chewing paper; he thinks he's a dog.

The letter was from a solicitor, telling me that Gerda had died, that it had happened several weeks ago. That stout bustling nephew had not bothered to tell me, when he must have known I would have wanted to come to the funeral. But I had stopped visiting so he had obviously written me off. Gerda would never have done that. She would have understood about my troubles.

There was a cheque inside the letter. She had left me a legacy of five thousand pounds. How wonderful it felt, just then. The money would take me to Alabama to see my granddaughter, to India too, to find Nicholas. There was another item which, the solicitor explained, they would arrange to be delivered to my house, a Jaeger coat, a coat the colour of strawberries.

Geoffrey was restless. He had seen something interesting under a cupboard. I set him down on the tiles and went to the window, needing to look at something green. That expanse of simple lawn with its old bird bath has often helped me at such moments, its very greenness has been like an ointment, gently spread over my eyes. I must have grass in my new garden, lots of grass, and trees.

So, I thought as I gazed, Gerda knows all things now. She has put away her childish things, her theatre of card and her biscuit cutter, her wall hangings from mysterious lands, her leather books. She is in the unknown region. Perhaps she will meet with my brother who is dead.

That night I dreamed about him. He had gone back to his old college for some special reunion. I never visited him in his student days so I do not know what his college was like but this event was happening in a great turretted

Victorian mansion set amongst pleasant grounds. A choked motorway, perhaps the M25, cut across one corner, but, as he closed the door on the outside, the noise of the traffic died away. Inside a feast was taking place, long benches with settles pulled up to them, hundreds of people engaged in talk, food and drink, black-and-white waitresses going round with bottles.

For a time Michael hesitated. He was never a confident person. When our mother sent us down to the village shop he used to hide behind me. In the dream he eventually went forward and said to an elderly woman 'Excuse me, but have you seen my friends?' Then he added, like an afterthought, 'And my family?'

The woman beamed at him and waved her glass for more wine because a hovering waitress looked in danger of moving on. 'No, I can't say that I have, but they are definitely here somewhere. Why don't you join us? There's plenty of room.' And she made a space on the bench for him.

I watched Michael sit down. I watched him take up a knife and a fork and begin to eat. I watched him drink some of the wine. And I went away not worrying, because the people he loved were there somewhere and this knowledge had seemed to be enough for him.

Perhaps, in the unknown region, time is different from here, and what we need, and what gives us joy. I mean, Michael could well have met Gerda by now, and his friends, and our mother and father, because the woman told him that everybody was there somewhere. But if he doesn't meet them it will be because it doesn't matter, so it will be all right.

Is that how it will be?

I might ask Marge.

Notes About the Authors:

Michael Carson has written a number of novels including *Sucking Sherbert Lemons* and *Stripping Penguins Bare*, and a collection of short stories, *Serving Suggestions*. He contributes a column to the weekly *Catholic Times*.

Alice Thomas Ellis has contributed a polemical column to Britain's *Catholic Herald* for many years. Of her many novels *The 27th Kingdom* was shortlisted for the Booker Prize, the trilogy *The Clothes in the Wardrobe, The Skeleton in the Cupboard* and *The Fly in the Ointment* were filmed as *The Summerhouse*, and *The Inn at the End of the World* won the Writers Guild Award for fiction.

Pauline Fisk's first novel, *Midnight Blue*, won the Smarties Prize for children's books. She is the author of several other successful children's novels, including *Telling the Sea*.

Frances Fuller lived for eighteen years through the hell of the bitter civil war in Lebanon. Her powerful first collection of short stories, *The Chameleon's Wedding Day*, published in 1996, reflects on this experience.

Jane Gardam is an English novelist and short-story writer for adults and children. *God On the Rocks*, which has been televised, was short-listed for the Booker Prize. She has worked as a journalist and editor.

Rumer Godden has written a large number of successful novels over a long writing careeer which she began in India before independence. *Black Narcissus*, about nuns struggling to establish a mission in the Himalaya region of India, was her first major success and subsequently became a highly regarded film. She has written for children as well as adults, producing classics such as *The Greengage Summer, The Diddakoi* and *The Peacock Spring*.

Graham Greene is considered to be one of the greatest twentieth-century English novelists. Among his best known novels are *Brighton Rock, The Power and the Glory, The Heart of the Matter, The End of the Affair* and *The Quiet American*.

Sara Maitland is a highly regarded feminist novelist, whose works include *Daughter of Jerusalem, Virgin Territory, Three Times Table* and *Home Truths*. Exploring the territory between fiction and theology she has also written *A Big Enough God* and *Angel and Me*.

Ann Pilling has written two novels, *A Broken Path* which was short-listed for the 1992 *Deo Gloria* prize, and *Considering Helen*. She has also written prolifically for children. *Henry's Leg* won the Guardian Award in 1986.

Adrian Plass is known for humorous books such as *The Sacred Diary of Adrian Plass Aged 37 3/4* and *Cabbages for the King*. He started writing following a stress-related illness in 1984.

J.F. Powers first achieved a reputation with his stories of the various lives of the Catholic clergy of the American Midwest in *Prince of Darkness* and *The Presence of Grace*. His novel *Morte D'Urban* won a National Book Award.

William Trevor is a master of the short story form and has won many prizes for his fiction, including the Whitbread Prize in 1994 for his novel *Felicia's Journey*.

Tim Winton is the author of thirteen books, including novels, a collection of stories, non-fiction and books for children. His first novel, *An Open Swimmer*, won the Australian/Vogel Prize. More recently *Cloudstreet* won the Banjo Award and Miles Franklin Award in Australia and the *Deo Gloria* Prize in the UK, and in 1995 *The Riders* was short-listed for the Booker Prize.

Acknowledgments

We would like to thank all those who have given us permission to include short stories in this book, as indicated in the list below. Every effort has been made to trace and contact copyright owners. If there are any inadvertent omissions or errors in the acknowledgements, we apologize to those concerned and will remedy these in the next edition.

Curtis Brown Group Ltd: 'Sister Malone and the Obstinate Man', copyright © Rumer Godden.
Laura Cecil Literary Agency: 'A Fool For Love, After All', copyright © 1996 Pauline Fisk.
Frances Fuller: 'Friends, Strangers, Brothers', copyright © 1996.
David Higham Associates Ltd: 'The Meeting House' from *Going into a Dark House*, published by Sinclair-Stevenson, copyright © Jane Gardam.
David Higham Associates Ltd: 'The Hint of an Explanation' by Graham Greene from *Twenty One Stories* published by Heinemann
David Higham Associates Ltd: 'Lantern Stalk' from *Blood and Water*, published by Pan, copyright © Tim Winton.
Kingsway Publications: 'Except Ye Become...' from *The Final Boundary*, published by Kingsway Publications, copyright © 1987, 1990 Adrian Plass
Sara Maitland: 'Jacob's Ladder', copyright © Sara Maitland
Penguin Books Ltd: 'The Statue' from pp 83–91 of *The Evening of Adam* by Alice Thomas Ellis, published by Viking 1994. Copyright © Alice Thomas Ellis 1994. Reproduced by permission of Penguin Books Ltd
Ann Pilling: 'Towards the Unknown Region', copyright © 1996.
Random House UK Ltd: 'The Forks' from *Prince of Darkness and Other Stories*, published by Chatto and Windus, copyright © J.F. Powers.
Richard Scott Simon Ltd: 'Even the Mice Know' from *Serving Suggestions*, published by Victor Gollancz. Copyright © 1993 Michael Carson.
William Trevor: 'Death in Jerusalem', copyright © William Trevor